# JUST FOR US

## WILD FIRE SERIES

# J.H. CROIX

*For my sweet B; for those who've loved a pet so much, they'd write them into a story; and for the ones who love woo-woo birds and who feel less alone in the quiet.*

# Chapter One

# KINCAID GREENE

"Hey, man." Hudson clapped me on the shoulder as he stopped beside me. "Want a beer? It's open bar," he added with a brow waggle.

A chuckle rustled in my throat. "Crazy, really."

"It's not like Fireweed Industries doesn't have money to waste," he pointed out. "So far, they only had a soft launch for this place. This is the official opening," he pointed out.

"I even heard of Fireweed Winery & Brewery in Minnesota," I replied.

"It's the biggest name in Alaska when it comes to any kind of corporation. They were ahead of the curve when it came to the whole craft beers and wine thing. Anyway, how are you liking Alaska so far?" he asked.

I paused for a beat before nodding. "Love it. I'm used to long winters, so I'm not worried about that. It's damn pretty country too."

Just then, Parker Reeves approached.

"Ah, here's the man of honor," Hudson said.

Parker, another firefighter on the hotshot crew I'd taken a position with recently, paused beside us, looking bemused. "You don't need to overdo it," he teased. This event was to honor Parker and his fiancée, Luna.

"Dude, you have a love story for the ages," Beck Steele commented as he stopped beside our group.

I'd quickly discovered Beck, a firefighter on another crew in town, was deeply in love with his wife and totally into everyone else being in love.

"For the ages?" I prompted.

Beck nodded, his gaze sobering. "Totally, man. They met one day when they were both in high school, walked on the beach, and kissed. And, here we are now. How much later?" He paused, glancing toward Parker.

Parker's lips curled in a bemused smile. "It's been a little over a decade."

"And, you didn't even know her name back then," Beck added.

Parker chuckled. "I do now."

"It was fate," Beck said, his voice laced with teasing conviction. He swung his attention to me. "What about you, Kincaid?"

"What about me?" I countered.

"I know you're new to the area and from Minnesota, so you can totally handle winter here. But what's your status? Girlfriend? Wife? Boyfriend? Husband?"

A laugh slipped out. "Uh, none of the above."

"What brought you here?" Beck asked.

"On my mom's bucket list to live here again."

"Really?" Hudson chimed in.

"Yep. She was in the Air Force when she was younger and stationed nearby. She always wanted to come back. So here we are."

"You are a good son." Beck's typically teasing gaze was somber.

"Well, I try," I offered with a light shrug.

"How's your mom doing?" he asked.

"Uh..." I paused, because, unbeknownst to him, that was a

loaded question. She was okay, but she had lupus and was dealing with a cluster of medical complications as a result. But that was a conversation for another day. "She's good," I said simply. She was good in spirits, and that was really all that mattered.

"Excellent. Well, when you meet, I don't know, the man or woman of your dreams, let me know. I'll give you all the advice you need," Beck said.

Parker rolled his eyes, hard. "You know, Beck, you're not the only guy here who's a family man and happy about it."

"Beck's the office gossip, always in everybody's business," Hudson interjected dryly.

Luna approached, and Parker immediately curled his arm around her shoulders, snugging her close against his side. He leaned down to give her a lingering kiss.

The love between them practically shimmered in the air around them. I wasn't prone to being a sappy, romantic guy, but in this moment, there was no doubt these two were happy together.

Conversation floated around us with congratulations to Parker and Luna punctuating many comments. The event in question had been thrown by the fire station, the crews all pitching in together to organize it with a big assist from Fireweed Winery because they were having their grand opening and thought it would be perfect to celebrate the couple's engagement along with it.

I loved Willow Brook and Alaska so far. I was even more pleased to be on the crew here. When you're a hotshot firefighter, you learn there's a certain mindset required. It takes a lot of nerve and a lot of confidence, and sometimes those qualities could translate into arrogance, which wasn't healthy for the work. The tone set here didn't brook that kind of attitude. Everyone had each other's backs, and I liked it.

I still wondered if my mother's hopes for our move to Alaska would ever come to fruition. But that was also a topic for another day, or rather, a question. One that had feathered in the back of my thoughts for most of my life.

"Hi guys," a voice said, and I glanced over, my gaze locking with a stunning pair of hazel eyes set off by glossy dark bangs framing the waitress's pretty face.

It wasn't as if I hadn't seen a beautiful woman before, but this one elicited a startling jolt. My thoughts swirled with curiosity, but all she was doing was checking to see if we needed any drinks.

# Chapter Two

# TORI SHACKLEFORD

The pace that evening at work was busy on steroids. For the most part, the eddy of customers flowed around me, creating a low hum. Until one moment. I was stunned into silence when I locked eyes with a man, one I'd never seen before. Shaggy, honey-brown hair, rich cognac eyes.

*Of course* he was a firefighter. There was a surplus of them here in Willow Brook.

I wanted to know his name, but I was working. When I hurried by him later, he caught my eye again, and his lips quirked at the corners. My belly responded with a shimmy and twist.

———

*A few days later*

I sat down on a large boulder, letting out a happy sigh. It was just me, myself, and my old dog, Bella. She promptly began sniffing everything she could, every grain of sand, every rock, pieces of seaweed, the ocean water lapping at the sand, the air, all of it. My dog knew how to be fully present in a moment.

"Home," I said aloud.

Willow Brook *was* home, along with Alaska and this little spot on the beach here. When I was a little girl, my mom used to take me here for walks, for frolicking, for rock hunting, and more.

Looking for a distraction, I leaned down, scooping up a piece of lava rock, my favorite kind of rock. They were lightweight and always seemed as if they'd been dropped here from another galaxy. This one was a deep burgundy color on one side that transitioned into black on the other. I lightly tossed it back and forth in my hands before setting it down on the boulder, planning to take it home with me.

I sat on that boulder for a little while, savoring the salty air and the birds chattering above the shoreline before I called Bella back. She was mostly deaf, but if I managed to make eye contact when I said her name, she came right over. She was a medium-sized brown dog with a half-tail. It wasn't purposefully docked like some, but literally about half length with kind of an angle on the end. The vet's best guess was she got it trapped in something.

Bella was my shadow, my soul dog. She went everywhere with me and was as loyal as a dog could be. Just as I got in the car, I heard a buzzing sound and glanced over to see some kind of bee flying straight for me. I yelled and swatted at it, but it zoomed right back and stung me just above my collarbone.

"Asshole!" I pointlessly hollered.

A few minutes later, I was driving back toward Willow Brook, toward home. The last thing I recalled was Bella letting out a sharp, unexpected bark. I woke up to the sound of the tail-end of my own yelp.

"There she is," a rumbling voice said.

I fought through layers of confusion and tried to drag in a deep breath, but my throat felt unbelievably tight. "Take it easy," the voice said. "You're in the middle of an anaphylactic reaction. The antihistamine shot should be taking effect. Give it a few minutes, and you'll be able to breathe a little better."

I dragged my eyes open and looked around wildly. I felt funny all over, and my throat was itchy and scratchy.

"Your dog is a good girl," the man said when I finally managed to focus on his face.

Holy wow. Even though I was half out of it, I knew a handsome man when I saw one. This guy was all handsome. His concerned brown eyes held mine. "How are you doing?"

My mind distantly clocked that I'd seen him at work the other night. He seemed professional. He was kneeling in the open driver's side door of my car with what appeared to be a bag with medical supplies on the ground.

"Did I pass out while I was driving?" I took another breath and discovered the tightness was loosening in my throat. I got more oxygen this time, and the fog in my brain started to clear.

Bella was beside me, her chin on my thigh. "I'm guessing you got stung by something." He lightly tapped his fingertip right where that stupid bee, or whatever, had stung me.

"Yeah, right before I got in my car. I've been stung before," I said slowly, as my thoughts started to organize themselves a little more coherently.

"Most people don't have a reaction until their second sting," he said. "You slid off the road, and your dog here started barking up a storm. I had my windows down nearby and heard her."

"Oh," I said brilliantly. "Are you an EMT?" I asked a moment later.

He was tucking things away in his bag. His gaze lifted to mine again. Although apparently, I had almost just died from anaphylactic shock, butterflies tickled my belly when his rich chocolate gaze snagged mine. His shaggy brown hair fell over his eyes. He had a straight nose, strong cheekbones that angled down to molded lips, and a square jaw with a little dimple at the base of his chin.

His lips kicked up at one corner and, holy hell, another dimple peeked out. "I'm a hotshot firefighter, not officially an EMT, but we all have first responder training, it's kinda part of the job."

My lips still felt a little funny, and I pressed them together quickly, relieved that the numbness and tingling were starting to wear off. "You can't throw a rock in Willow Brook without hitting a hotshot firefighter," I managed to tease.

He chuckled, and the sound spun through me, sending my belly into a swoop. "True," he said as he tipped his head to the side.

He leaned back, and I was abruptly disappointed to have him move away from me. "Are you leaving now?" Alarm shot through me with a burst of dizzying anxiety on its heels. I had just passed out in my car by myself with my dog.

"I'm not leaving," he replied, his tone easygoing. "You shouldn't drive for a while. Also, when you drove off the road, you collided with a boulder."

"What?" I shook my head, trying to think. "Is my car okay?"

"Mostly. You have a small scratch on your bumper, but you also have a flat tire and a bent rim. I'll give you a ride. To be on the safe side, we should probably take you to the hospital to get you checked out."

"Oh, no, no, no." I waved a hand in the air, the motion wobbly. "I'm fine, right? You gave me a shot, and I'm all set," I protested.

"Am I going to have to be official and insist?" He looked genuinely concerned, his gorgeous brown eyes studying me.

I let out a sigh. "Fine, I'll go." Bella nudged my knee with her nose, and I absently stroked her head.

Eventually, he helped me out of the car. It was not a bad deal *at all* to have his strong hands guiding me up and out. He kept an arm around my shoulders to help keep me steady as I walked up the slight incline to his truck.

Bella was practically glued to my calves. He insisted on

helping me into his passenger seat and buckling me in. Maybe it was because I was a little out of it, but when he leaned over to buckle my seatbelt, I almost kissed him.

Once I was situated, he opened the back door and lifted Bella into the back. She immediately poked her head in between the seats and licked my elbow.

He chuckled. "She takes good care of you."

"Bella is my family," I said simply as I leaned over and gave her a kiss on top of her head.

His lips quirked at the corners. "Good to know her name."

I tried to carry on a conversation on the drive to the hospital, but I was still hazy. I learned his name was Kincaid. He'd recently moved to Willow Brook when he accepted a position on one of the hotshot crews here. He was from somewhere in the lower 48, but I couldn't remember where.

We got into a little standoff in the parking lot at the hospital when he wanted to put me in a wheelchair and wheel me in. I refused. "No."

When his lips twitched at the corners, I felt all tingly inside.

Without a word, he curled an arm around my waist and walked me inside. When we stopped in front of the circular desk, a familiar face looked up at me. "Tori!"

"Holly?"

Holly grinned. "I heard you were back in town and that you've been working at Fireweed Winery, but I haven't seen you." Her eyes shifted to Kincaid. "Is she okay?"

# Chapter Three

# KINCAID

Tori let out a put-upon sigh. "I'm fine." She thumbed toward me. "Kincaid insisted I come here. I got stung by a bee and ran into a boulder —" She shrugged as if it was no big deal that she almost went into anaphylactic shock and drove off the road.

"I stopped to check on her because—"

Before I could finish, Holly jumped in, "Of course you stopped! You're a good man."

"I gave her a shot of epinephrine and suggested she get cleared here."

Holly nodded briskly, all business as her gaze swept over Tori. "That's protocol. We'll check you over, and we can send you home with something that'll keep that allergic reaction from flaring back up."

"I don't understand. I've been stung before," Tori explained.

"It's not unusual for people to have a reaction the second time they get stung. Come on back with me." Holly bustled out from behind the desk just as another nurse stopped beside her. She glanced over at the man. "Chris, remember Tori? She just moved back to town. She got stung by something, and her car made friends with a rock." Chris snorted at that. "You hold down the fort for a few minutes while I check her out."

Chris brought his attention to Tori with a smile. "Hey, Tori, remember me from high school?"

Tori smiled weakly as she nodded. "I do. It's nice to see you, Chris."

A moment later, we followed Holly down the hallway. "This is like a reunion," Tori murmured.

Holly tossed a grin over her shoulder, her blond ponytail swinging. "It is! I'm glad you didn't get hurt when you slid off the road," Holly added as we walked into an exam room. "How bad was it?" She glanced toward me.

"Her front tire kissed the boulder. All in all, just a scratch on her bumper and a bent tire rim, which created a flat tire. That's why I brought her here."

Holly began checking Tori's vitals, and I took the moment to study her. Her glossy, almost-black hair was twisted into a braid. Several long strands had fallen around her cheeks, framing her strong, angled cheekbones. Just beneath her mussed bangs was a pair of wide hazel eyes, green shot through with gold and brown. It was like looking into a forest. Her skin was sun-kissed with a rosy tint to it. Standing, she was almost as tall as me with a strong athletic build.

When Holly turned away to do something, Tori's gaze locked with mine. In a fiery second, it felt like the air was scorched from the heat that sizzled between us. My cells spun and tightened.

*Dude, now is not the time or place to get hot over this woman.*

My mind had a point, but my body had a stronger opinion. Tori carried this spark, an independence woven through with a steely attitude that revved my engine. Not to mention, she was flat-out stunning. She had a fresh cheeked, understated beauty. Her strong, angled cheekbones were paired with a straight nose, almost aristocratic, and full, sensual lips.

When she held her arm out for Holly to put the blood pressure cuff on, I noticed the lines of a tattoo peeking out from underneath the edge of her T-shirt sleeve.

Holly glanced over at me. "All looks good. I'm still going to send her home with an antihistamine prescription to prevent her reaction from flaring up again. What's the plan with her car?"

"The plan was for me to bring her here." I chuckled. "I can take her to the pharmacy and drop her off at home. We can call the local mechanic shop to pick up your car and deal with your tire," I said, glancing back at Tori.

Tori let out a puff of breath to blow her bangs out of her eyes. "You don't have to do that."

"I don't mind at all."

Holly smiled at Tori. "Kincaid's a firefighter. They do helpful things like that. Plus, what else are you going to do about your car if you don't do that?"

"I suppose you have a point," Tori replied dryly.

Holly waggled her brows before turning to type some information into her laptop. A short while later, after Tori had called to have her car towed and been cleared to leave, we picked up her medication at the pharmacy. Bella's short tail was thumping against the back seat when we turned into the driveway where Tori had directed me.

"How are you feeling?" I asked as I rolled to a stop in front of a small house.

Her eyes met mine with a sheepish smile. "I'm fine. Thank you for everything today. In hindsight, I realize this could've been really serious if you hadn't gotten there as soon as you did."

As I held her gaze, it felt as if sparks were shimmering in the air. Bella poked her head between us, licking my forearm and my chin, drawing a laugh out of me.

"Bella likes you," Tori offered.

"I love dogs. She's a sweetie, and I'm glad she made some noise earlier."

"Do you live near where I drove off the road?" she asked.

"I do. I heard Bella when I stopped to check my mail."

The urge to kiss Tori was strong, but that was fucking insane. I forced myself to climb out of my truck and fetch the bag she'd tucked behind the seat. A moment later, Bella was trotting along at Tori's side as we walked up to the house.

We stopped in front of the door, and I glanced over. "Is this your house?"

"It is."

It suddenly felt like a whole lot of emotions were crowding the space between us. Tori started to say something just as a moose appeared. It was a bull moose with a large pair of antlers. He was snorting as he trotted by, paying zero attention to us. Out of the corner of my eye, motion caught my attention. Another moose barreled out of the trees so fast that Bella barked.

Tori turned, her foot slipping on the gravel. For the second time today, I caught her in my arms. Just when I wondered if we were in for a moose trampling, the pair of moose snorted at each other and raced into the trees.

Tori looked up at me. Her palm had landed right over my heart, and I had no doubt she could feel the rapid beat of it.

"Bella!" she called when Bella began to run after the moose. Her hand fell away as she stepped back.

I'd already gathered that Bella was old, but at her pace, there was absolutely no way she could catch up to those moose. Blessedly, she stopped and looked over her shoulder at Tori before turning and walking back.

Tori looked up at me one last time, her pretty eyes locking with mine. "Thank you. Again."

"Anytime. If you need a ride to pick up your car tomorrow, just text me."

The next day, I stared down at Kincaid's number, contemplating that I really didn't have anybody else to call for a ride.

Of course, I'd grown up here and knew plenty of people, but most of them I hadn't seen in years. I definitely didn't have their cell numbers. There was also the giant ball of one ugly drama that marred my history here. When I'd left for college, I'd all but kicked up dust behind me in the wake of escaping the gossip swirling around my family.

I tapped Kincaid's contact information.

———

"Got it," I called as I lifted the tray of drinks and hustled out to deliver them.

I loved my job. Maybe for some people, being a waitress at a winery and restaurant wasn't all that, but I loved the hustle and bustle. I practically never looked at the clock. With it being summer in Alaska, there wasn't a single day here at Fireweed Winery and Restaurant that wasn't wall-to-wall customers with tourists crowding Alaska.

"This mead is amazing," a woman said as I delivered the second round of drinks to their table.

I glanced at the bottle. "Yes, the blueberry mead is—" I pinched my fingers together and blew a kiss. "Chef's kiss. One of my favorites, to be honest. Would you all like dessert?" I whisked my gaze around the group of women.

"I shouldn't, but yes," one of the women said.

"We're celebrating everything," another chimed in.

"Everything?" I prompted.

"It's a divorce trip," another offered.

"You came to Alaska to celebrate a divorce?"

"Yes!" one of the women said, thrusting her fist into the air. On the heels of that, they all raised their glasses and clinked them together.

"Okay, so this divorce is worthy of celebration?" I teased.

They nodded vigorously. They were a pleasure to wait on— friendly, funny, and full of questions. This was clearly a good group of friends.

"Whose divorce are you celebrating?" I asked.

"Mine!" the woman who had thrust her hand into the air said.

"Well, your dessert's on the house," I said.

She took a deep breath, blinking just as I saw what I thought was a flash of pain in her eyes. "So, what are our options then?"

I quickly rattled off the dessert menu, having it memorized by heart. "And, tonight's dessert special is a blueberry cheesecake with blueberry drizzle. Also, chef's kiss. Blueberries are in season, if you didn't catch that detail," I said dryly.

They all went with the blueberry cheesecake.

"Thank God I don't have to listen to Brad bitch about my weight," the divorcee said.

I eyed her. "You look amazing. I'm not flirting or anything. I'm just objectively offering that observation. Your ex sounds like a jerk."

"Ava is adorable!" one of her friends—slightly tipsy—exclaimed.

The entire group giggled.

"Well, no one needs to be married or date anyone who has anything to say about their body that isn't good, right? We celebrate the female form," another one of the friends said.

Ava looked a little teary as her eyes arced about the table. She lifted her gaze to mine. "It wasn't just that he bitched about how I looked. It was that when I found out he was cheating on me, he said it was because I was getting a little chubby. Do I look chubby to you?" She gestured up and down.

"Not at all," I said firmly. She looked healthy and curvy, and beautiful. "You look amazing, and it's all for the best. This is a perfect trip for a divorce trip, or whatever this is."

"Thank you." She beamed up at me, seeming to have recovered from the earlier flicker of hurt.

I got swept into the rest of the evening, as was always the case, but I couldn't help checking on them one last time as I brought the check. I caught Ava's gaze.

"It's all up from here," I told her.

"It is, right?" she pressed.

I nodded. "Absolutely." I smiled at her, lightly squeezing her shoulder. "We all deserve to be treated well. That's not too much to ask."

They left me a wildly extravagant tip, which I didn't discover until after they had gone. The night wound down. I appreciated the later part of these evenings—wiping down the tables, putting things away, and so on. It gave me a chance to wind down after the usually hectic pace. I was just finishing up in the back. The kitchen was quiet, with the soft sounds of clinking and cleaning and the hum of the industrial-sized dishwasher, when I heard Tish's voice.

"How's it going, Tori?" she asked.

I glanced over. "Awesome. Another busy night."

"Is it ever not busy?" Tish mused dryly, her eyes twinkling.

I grinned as I untied my apron and tossed it in the laundry basket in the corner of the break area.

"Definitely not. What are you doing here so late?"

Tish Cannon managed the administrative side of things for Fireweed Industries for the location here in Willow Brook. When I was growing up here, they'd had a mine that shut down at some point. Eventually, they revamped it into a renewable energy business after reopening the offices. Somewhere along the way, someone had decided it would also be smart to open up a winery and restaurant—like their flagship location in Fireweed Harbor, in Southeast Alaska. These additions were nothing but good news for Willow Brook, as far as bringing business and tourists to town.

"Oh, Griffin and I had dinner here, and he's out there talking with his cousin, Archer. So, you know me, I had to do a loop."

"A loop?" I teased.

She shrugged lightly, a sheepish smile on her face. "Just check in and see how it's going."

"How is Teddy doing?" I asked, referring to her toddler-aged son.

"Allie, Graham's daughter, is babysitting."

"Must be nice to have a night out," I commented.

Tish tipped her head to the side. "Yes, but it's always weird. If you ever have kids, you'll see what I mean." Pausing, she held a hand up. "Not that you have to have kids. Kids aren't everything."

I shrugged. "I don't actually know if I want to have kids. Although they're sure cute, but they seem like a lot of work."

"Oh, they are a shit-ton of work." Tish nodded firmly. With a glance at her watch, she added," I should rustle Griffin up."

"Always good to see you, Tish."

Tish wasn't technically my boss. She didn't have much to do with the running of the restaurant, but she did sign my paychecks as the admin person in HR.

"You should come out for card night. You keep not coming," she said.

"What do you mean?" I hedged.

"Just that. I've invited you three times, and three times you vague-boop your way out of it."

"Tish!" I exclaimed, trying to ignore the prick of defensiveness inside.

"It's at Holly's place next week." Her smile was warm.

"Text me the details. I'll come."

She texted me on the spot, just as Griffin appeared at her side. Her husband was one of the Cannon family who owned Fireweed Industries. It was the biggest business in Alaska, and it even made the news here and there since it was an international corporation. It still surprised me that Griffin had been a hotshot firefighter—and still did that on occasion—even though he also worked for the family business. They had money. Lots of it. I suppose when you were one of six siblings, maybe you wanted to strike out on your own.

"Sweetheart," he murmured, sliding an arm around Tish's waist.

She blushed a little when he pressed a kiss to her cheek, and my heart twisted sharply in my chest with an old pain. I was always happy for anyone who was happily in love, but it still felt like something impossible for me. It was safe to say trust was hard to come by for me.

"I gotta run," I said, offering a quick smile between them. "Have a good night. Good to see you, Griffin," I called as I spun and hurried away.

When I got home, Bella was sound asleep, so deaf that she didn't hear me until I got right up to her. The vet had told me she probably felt the vibration of my footsteps on the floor.

She wagged her little tail, looking a little tired, as she lumbered up to her feet. I wanted her to live forever. She was still mostly healthy and had a strong heart, but I didn't know how much longer I'd have her.

Between the divorce party group tonight and that little pinch of seeing the way Griffin looked at Tish, Bella reminded me of what was pure and true—a dog's love. No strings. No mess. No complications. No lies. I could always trust in that.

Chapter Five

# TORI

I stood at the counter in Firehouse Café. It was quiet and early, so there weren't many people here yet. Casey was busy filling the display case with fresh baked goods. Luna had peered out from the kitchen in the back to say good morning. She and I had actually gone to elementary school together, but she'd left before my family imploded.

Sometimes I wondered just how much the implosion had been felt by anyone else. In a small town, gossip could burn hot and fast. It had been quite the bomb dropped for everyone to learn that my father, a beloved police officer, had been having a long-time affair. For over a decade. With my mom's best friend.

My mom hadn't known. I hadn't known. Until I walked in on them. That was *so* not fun.

The aftermath was a mess. To this day, I still carried lingering anger with my father. The trust rupture for my mom had been massive. My dad and Shelly had left town. He took a job in Anchorage. Of course, he had another affair later. Now, Shelly was busy trying to make it up to my mom, and my mom was busy ignoring her. After all of it, I was proud of my mom. She was still here. She was the reason I'd moved back.

"Well, hello, Tori," Janet James said.

My eyes lifted to see Janet, the heart of Firehouse Café and maybe the whole town. "Hey!" I exclaimed.

Her eyes twinkled. "What can I get you?"

"Coffee and a raspberry scone. Also, a hug."

Janet's smile was wide as she rounded the counter to pull me into one of her comforting hugs.

After that, she put a scone in the warmer and began to prep my coffee. "I haven't seen you here when I've been in yet. What gives?" I asked.

"I still own the café, but Luna manages it now. You know that, right?"

"Well, I actually didn't know that. I've only been back in town for a little while. Is everything okay?" I tried not to sound too worried.

"Oh, yes! I just need to slow down a little. When Luna started baking donuts for me, I realized she might be a good fit to take over. Her donuts are divine."

"Ah, well, excellent plan. Do we call them Divine Donuts?" I teased.

"Just Luna's donuts," Janet said with a smile. "You've met Casey, right?" she asked, gesturing to Casey, who stopped at her side.

"She's waited on me a few times," I replied. "But I don't think we've gotten past names." I grinned over at Casey. "Born and raised in Willow Brook, and I'm back."

"So you have credibility," Casey teased.

"Is that what we call it??"

Casey shrugged lightly. "I've only made it through one winter so far. I can't call myself an Alaskan until I'm an old hand at winter."

"Ah. The winters are a thing. Where are you from originally?"

"Coastal North Carolina. It's freaking hot there. I love the snow here. It's so pretty. I love how it brightens everything up." She tipped her head to the side. "Are you glad to be back?"

I paused, contemplating. "I missed Willow Brook." This was true, but my feelings were complex around my hometown.

"Why did you leave?"

"The usual. College and so on." I figured vague-booking it was the best way to explain. "I haven't been that far away. I went to college in Juneau."

"Oh, so you're Alaskan through and through." Casey nodded thoughtfully.

Janet slid my coffee across the counter. I lifted it, taking a swallow immediately. "Oh, so good."

Janet got swept into serving other customers, as did Casey. I slipped out of the way to wait for the scone I'd ordered. When the bell chimed on the door, I glanced over, and instantly, my stomach plunged. My mother's former best friend glanced over, and our eyes met.

Shelly had babysat me so many times growing up. Her daughter and I had been friends. Maybe not best friends, but we'd been babysat back and forth between our parents. Until the whole messy, ugly, and hurtful truth came out.

While Shelly smiled at me, dread coiled inside my chest and I couldn't even force a polite smile. As soon as Janet's eyes landed on Shelly, her gaze whipped toward me. Of course, Janet knew the whole story. Even worse, it spread through high school because when the entire drama came out—that Shelly had been having an affair with my dad, her best friend's husband, for a whole-ass decade, and my mom had left him. Shelly and my dad moved in together and left town not long after that. Oh, so much fun.

Shelly was trying hard to somehow mend the bridges that she had literally thrown grenades at before. Good fucking grief, I could *not* tolerate her trying to be friends with my mother and me. It was all too much.

Over she came anyway. "Hi, Tori." Her smile was soft, a little tremulous. "How are you? I heard you moved back to town."

"Seriously, Shelly?" was all I said.

"What can I get you, Shelly?" Casey said brightly, blessedly interrupting.

"My usual," Shelly said, her tone cool.

I immediately didn't like that she wasn't being nice enough to Casey, by my standards, at least. I stayed quiet and took the warm scone Luna passed over. I hadn't even noticed her come out from the back.

"Do you need anything?" Luna asked, her voice low.

"An escape hatch?" I quipped.

"Do you want to come in the back?"

"I'll take you up on that," I whispered.

"You can meet my dog," she said brightly, her voice rising.

"Well, I love dogs," I said, already moving in her direction.

With another glance at Shelly, while I could practically feel her eyes burning holes into my shoulder blades, I rounded the counter and followed Luna into the back of the café.

"You know, I've never been back here," I commented.

Luna grinned. "Most people don't come back here unless they work here. Or unless Janet drags you back here, or me."

"Thank you." I took a breath, mentally sagging inside. "Are you glad you moved back?" I asked, trying not to think about Shelly.

"One hundred percent. I missed it," Luna said firmly.

"How long were you away?"

"If you didn't hear, my parents moved us away to be RV influencers. It totally sucked. If I had my way, we never would've left, but I didn't have my way. So now I'm back," Luna explained.

"RV influencers?" I gave my head a little shake.

"Oh yeah. They drove all over Alaska, living in an RV and posting about our lives online. Were you lucky enough not to watch their channel?"

"I guess? Not really my thing."

"Good." She chuckled. She thumbed over her shoulder. "Shelly seems to be trying awful hard to make it up to pretty much everybody."

"I know," I murmured.

"Follow me to meet my dog." Luna led me through a back door, and we crossed the rear parking area into a separate building.

"What's this?" I asked curiously.

"An old garage that came with the property for the café. Jasmine has her pottery studio on that side," she added, peering through an inside window. "She's not working right now."

"And this is...?"

"Fuzzy," she said as a large white dog approached, tail swinging in a wide arc and tongue lolling. "He hangs out here when I'm working."

"Oh, he's the sweetest thing!" I knelt down to pet him, and Fuzzy circled me with his tail thumping against my sides. "I have an old dog. Her name's Bella. Maybe they could play together sometime. Her playing is pretty slow, but she loves other dogs. She always has."

I finally stood up from petting Fuzzy, and Luna walked me back to the café. "You can just cut over to the parking lot if you want," she pointed out.

I shook my head. "I refuse to let Shelly chase me away from places I want to be."

Luna was quiet for a beat before pulling me into an unexpected hug.

Stepping back, I sighed. "It's just... awkward, you know?"

"Oh, I do. One of the things I love about small towns is how people take care of each other. Nobody's a stranger. The flip side to that is everybody knows everybody's business, and sometimes that's super awkward."

I laughed softly. "It is. But life goes on, right?"

"It always does."

Luna stayed in the kitchen to bake, and I slipped back out front. I decided to do what I'd planned, which was to sit down and quietly enjoy my coffee and scone, even though Shelly was there, sitting by herself.

Grateful there were plenty of other customers around, I snagged a table. "Oh, well hey there, Tori." As soon as I heard that voice, my system jolted. It felt as if my libido was waking up like my old dog Bella, coming out of sleep abruptly and shaking off.

My cheeks were burning before my eyes even met his. "Oh, uh, hey, Kincaid." My voice was ridiculously breathless. His cognac gaze held mine. "What are you doing here?" I asked, rather pointlessly.

He lifted his coffee. "Getting coffee."

Out of the corner of my eye, I saw Shelly stand from her table. I didn't even want to risk her trying to come over and talk to me, so I blurted out, "Have a seat."

My invitation was enough out of the blue, and my tone bright enough, that Kincaid arched a brow. Yet, he sat right down without missing a beat. "Am I occupying this chair to keep it from someone else?" he asked.

My cheeks heated again, this time because I was a little embarrassed that he picked up on that. "Yeah," I said with a sheepish smile.

Shelly—bold as ever, apparently—stopped beside the table. "I'd love to talk sometime, Tori," she said.

I lifted my gaze to her, figuring if she was going to be bold, I might as well be too.

"I wouldn't, Shelly. Take care. If you don't mind, I'm having coffee with a friend."

Her lips pinched a little, a look familiar to me. That was what she did when her daughter and I were little, and she was annoyed with our behavior. "You take care," she finally said, her voice cool as she turned away.

"Okay," Kincaid said after a few beats, leaning back in his chair. "So there's a story there. What is it? What did she ever do to you?"

"She's my mother's *former* best friend. She used to babysit me all the time." I took a deep breath. "She had an affair with my dad. For a decade. Needless to say, my mom's not friends with her anymore, and I don't want to be friendly with her."

"Oh, *oh*," Kincaid said, his eyes widening slightly. "I understand."

"Then, they moved in together, and eventually they moved to Anchorage and got married. He went on to have an affair on her sometime after that. I guess she's come back to town and wants to make up with my mom and me." I shook my head, calling on the numbness I needed inside to keep from breaking into tears. "I'm not interested."

"Well, uh, I completely understand that." His tone was careful and level.

"All this to say, for what it's worth, I do have trust issues," I added with a wry chuckle.

Kincaid snorted, tilting his head to the side. The way his gaze softened twisted my heart with a piercing jolt. "Fair enough. Don't we all?"

I paused for a moment before shrugging. "I don't know. Maybe. What's your story?"

*Chapter Six*

# KINCAID

I guess we were just jumping right into the deep end in this conversation. The hurt in Tori's eyes was so sharp, I could feel the piercing twist of it in my own chest. She held my gaze expectantly.

"Maybe my dad didn't do that, but my dad just... Well, he didn't do the dad thing." I figured if she was going to offer honesty to me, I'd give her the same.

Tori took a swallow of her coffee, angling her head to the side as her pretty hazel eyes studied mine. Questions flickered there. "You mean your dad left?"

"He was never even there to have left. For all intents and purposes, he was a sperm donor," I explained evenly.

"Oh. Well, that sucks." She blinked, and the concern in her eyes warmed the cool feeling in my heart whenever I thought about my dad, or rather, his complete lack thereof in my life.

I shrugged, trying to reach for the lightness I used to ease that desolate sense of loneliness. It felt like a dry wind through a barren place, especially when there was no one around, a clanging sense of isolation. And yet, here we were in Alaska. My mother had other reasons for wanting to return, but she also wanted to maybe find him.

My mother had, as she put it, felt morally bound to let my sperm donor know she was pregnant. She'd never heard from him again after that.

"In a way, maybe it's easier than what you experienced," I added.

Tori shook her head quickly and definitively. "I don't think it's helpful to compare pain. It's all relative, I think."

I was quiet for a few beats, considering her point. "Maybe, maybe not. I don't know."

"There's a lot I don't know about life, but no one's helped by measuring pain on a yardstick. I'm sorry your father wasn't around." Her tone was straightforward, her gaze clear.

"Thank you," I said, meaning it. "Should we talk about something lighter now?" I asked, my tone dry as the dead grass after the snow melted in the spring.

She bit her lip, her smile sheepish. "Yes. Let's. That was kind of a heavy start."

"You look all recovered from your, uh, bee sting," I offered.

"I am. Thank you again."

"Anytime. I'm just glad you're okay and glad I happened to be there pretty quickly."

"Now that I know I'm allergic, I have to worry about getting stung again," she pointed out.

"Just carry an EpiPen."

"For real?" she pressed.

"Yeah. You can jab yourself."

Her eyes went wide. "That's what most people do?" At my nod, she wrinkled her nose. "Sheesh."

"Getting stung by an insect isn't that common, all things considered. If I happen to be around, I always have one on me," I pointed out.

"Are you allergic to something?"

"I'm a firefighter and first responder, so I keep those kinds of things around."

"Not a bad habit to have." Her lips curled a little at the corners.

"Well, because of that habit, I had one that afternoon."

She giggled. "Bella thanks you too."

"Your dog is an absolute sweetheart. How is she?"

"She's good. She's old."

"Old dogs are the best, aren't they?"

"Yeah." Tori's smile was bittersweet. "Absolutely. She likes to nap. She likes the sunshine. And, she likes me."

"All good things," I offered lightly.

"Hey, hey, hey," a voice interjected.

We glanced over together to see Beck and Maisie approaching. I might've only been in town for a little while, but Beck was easy to become friends with. Of course, I also knew Maisie well. She was the main dispatcher at Willow Brook Fire & Rescue.

"How's it going?" Beck said when they stopped by the table.

"Good. You?" Tori returned.

Beck tilted his head to the side, considering her question seriously. "Pretty good. Except we didn't sleep last night."

"Oh, yeah?" Tori's brow furrowed.

"Two kids with colds. Misery."

"Oof," Tori said.

"That's the only negative thing I've ever heard you say about being a dad," I teased lightly.

Maisie sighed. "Sick kids aren't great. We try to trade off, but you sleep like shit no matter what."

I studied him. "You actually look tired, Beck."

He met my gaze and let out a sharp sigh. "Fucking exhausted, man. But we're gonna get coffee, and it's all good."

"Where are the sick kids now?" Tori asked the obvious question.

"My mom's babysitting. Because she's a fucking saint," Beck said flatly.

Tori bit her lip to keep from laughing, but it slipped out

anyway. Maisie laughed along with her. "Beck's mom is so good to us."

"Someday, you might understand. It's all worth it," Beck insisted.

I shrugged. "Maybe."

After a little more casual conversation, they made their way up to get coffee. Tori took a slow swallow of her coffee before she studied me for a beat.

"Well, since we dove right into our trust baggage, what do you think about kids?"

"Kids?" I sputtered.

"Exactly," she said dryly.

"Exactly what?" I prompted.

"I can't imagine it. Too many variables."

"Can I ask you a question?" When the moment stretched between us, I added, "I guess we're covering all the territory now, and I'm not even sure why."

"Well, because..." she rolled her eyes. "Shelly." She scoffed and straightened in her chair. "What's your question?"

"Do you ever imagine yourself settling down?" I had no clue why I was asking her this. None at all.

Tori narrowed her eyes slightly, her teeth worrying her bottom lip, which sent a sizzling jolt of electricity through me. *Dude, you're having a serious conversation. Don't be lusting after this woman.*

"I don't know. Not really. I can't imagine it. I don't ever want to go through what my mom went through. You just never know what people are going to do. I loved my dad because you kind of can't un-love somebody. But he really hurt my mom, and he really hurt me. He passed away, and I never really got over what happened." She paused, her voice softening as she added, "He was like a pillar of the community, police officer and all that. People in town loved him. He was awesome as a dad. And yet, he was having an affair with my mom's best friend for ten years. Most of my childhood, really." She let out a sharp breath. "And, I still feel so stupid. Like I should've known somehow. Every now and then, I'd sense that there was tension between my parents, but I never really knew. I could *not* have imagined what he was doing."

I nodded slowly. "I understand. That must've been awful."

"What about you? Do you want to settle down?" she prompted.

The boomerang of my own question circled back to hit me with force. She hadn't been pointed, but my own issues felt sharp around this. "Uh... maybe. But I don't know. I don't have a model for a relationship. It's just always been me and my mom. My mom's awesome. But a relationship's never been high on my list. I'll be fine, with or without one. I'm happy for people like Maisie and Beck, and whoever else finds that kind of connection and wants to do the happy family dance. My mom was pretty happy on her own. She still is, and my life is going okay."

Tori nodded slowly, her gaze studying me quietly. After a moment, her lips quirked at the corners in a rueful smile. "I feel like we're on a date. You know, like those dating apps where you check off all the questions. I don't do those at all, but I tried a little bit in college, and I'm all set." She shuddered a little.

I chuckled. "I've never tried a dating app. I've heard too many nightmares about them."

I wanted to tell her that I wanted this to be a date.

But I didn't.

The following evening, I hustled from one table to the other. With it being spring, the pace of tourists was beginning to flow faster into town. I spun through the night. I was pretty much on autopilot—reeling off the specials, serving the drinks, getting the food, all the while laughing and joking and collecting plenty of tips.

In a rush, I moved from a big family table to a small table facing the windows. I didn't look up until I was standing by the table.

My eyes collided with Shelly's gaze. The woman who smiled through family barbecues with us for years. The woman who used to swear my mom's potato salad was the best. And, who, apparently, for a decade of those years, carried on an affair with my father. Here she was now. Maybe not happy—but here.

For a few extra seconds, I contemplated turning away and asking to have my section reassigned, but that meant making somewhat of a scene. Even though I knew it would be okay, that my boss would let it slide, I didn't feel like going through with it.

So, with my face feeling like it was about to crack and shatter into pieces at the effort, I smiled. I swallowed through the cold tightness in my throat and chest. I was holding it together. Just barely.

"What can I get you?" I asked politely.

Shelly's eyes met mine. Once upon a time, I'd known her so well. It wasn't just family barbecues. She had come over many a time in a pinch when my mom was busy at work. She was the one who brought me pads because my mom was at work once. She had cleaned up my knees when I scraped them. She had been the closest thing to a second mom that I ever had.

I despised what she had done to our family.

"Tori," she began.

I breathed through that cold tightness. "Shelly, I can't do this. I'm working. Let me just take your order."

"Look, just listen to me for a minute, and I'll order. But, please just listen." Seeing as I either walked away or listened, I stayed silent. "I really want a chance to talk to your mom, and she won't talk to me. It's like a wall."

My mouth actually fell open. "Shelly, are you serious? You were fucking my dad for a decade. My mom thought you were her friend. That's not what friends do. I'm sorry you're sad about blowing up your friendship, but you did it. It's all on you. All of it. Don't start with the whole 'well, there were some problems in their marriage' bullshit. Maybe there were. I have no idea. Really, it's hard to know when everything turns out to be a lie. It doesn't matter. That is a violation by an alleged friend that can't be papered over. So good luck with that. My mom's probably more forgiving than me." I took a slow breath, willing the anger burning through me to cool. "What can I get you?"

Blessedly, Shelly ordered nothing more than a drink. I retreated to the bar. My hands were shaking, and I could barely breathe.

I served her that drink, left her check at the table, and said nothing else. I didn't cry. I was really proud. I just kept working. Blessedly, it was late. I kept it all together until I made it out to the back patio toward the end of my shift—a staff-only section where they had recently put up decorative string lights in preparation for some events. They were glittering in the darkness.

I leaned against the railing, trying to breathe through the emotion bottled inside. With it being early spring, the air was still cool with a bite to it. Goosebumps rose on my arms. That coolness was better than the heat of anger that blasted through the cold numbness I felt whenever I even thought about Shelly and my dad.

I didn't even hear the footsteps. I didn't hear anything. Until I heard Kincaid's voice.

"Are you okay?" he asked quietly.

I spun around, curling my hands onto the railing at my sides. My nervous system was a jumble, all my nerves rattled from my encounter with Shelly.

I didn't want to talk, but Kincaid was here, his presence steady and solid. I didn't sense pressure from him. He just waited, like he'd stand there in this chilly evening for hours if that's what I needed.

Finally, my voice barely audible, I managed to say, "Shelly. Again." I shook my head.

"I wondered," he offered. "I saw her leaving."

Kincaid's expression didn't change much, but his eyes darkened, and I saw his jaw tighten just slightly. He stepped a little closer, close enough for me to feel his warmth emanating, his strength almost surrounding me.

I didn't expect him to say anything.

"Tori," he finally said. "You don't have to hold it together."

His words unraveled me. It was as if he had tugged lightly on the tiny threads barely holding me together. My eyes stung, just for a second. I blinked rapidly, and my breath caught in my throat. He reached out slowly, slow enough I could stop him if I wanted to. When his hand lifted to tuck a strand of hair behind my ear, I felt the brush of his fingertips on that sensitive skin along the shell of my ear.

It was quiet out here, the air around us crowded with

unspoken emotions. I could hear my own breath. The distant call of an owl, followed by a raven in the darkness. The sound of wings beating through the air passed by.

I finally looked up at him, really looked. The sense of emotion in me was so heightened, so fraught. I wanted anything to distract me from it. Here was Kincaid. A firefighter with all kinds of rescue-y vibes.

The space between us shifted, the air thickening. It felt charged—a humming pause, as if the air itself was holding its breath just as I was.

Kincaid leaned in, the motion incremental. Close enough that his warmth felt like tendrils of smoke curling around me. He didn't move again. He just waited.

I exhaled a small, shaky laugh. "How do you do this?"

"Do what?"

"Make me feel safe. Every time. I mean, it all started when you saved my life, so maybe that's it."

The rustle of the low chuckle in his throat sent goosebumps prickling over my skin. He smiled, his lips kicking up slightly.

"How do you make me feel like my life isn't on fire... when it is?" I whispered.

He tipped his head. "Well, you make me feel like it *is* on fire, but I'm not sure that's what you mean."

Heat pooled low in my belly, and I felt the strongest pull. My hand fell to his chest, where I could feel the rapid thump of his heart. I wasn't thinking, at all, when I leaned up and brought my lips to his. I wasn't sure what would happen, but he met me right there. His hand, palming my cheek.

I felt rare in this moment, fragile. Our lips brushed together once, and then again, his lingering on mine for a beat before he drew away. Just close enough for me to still feel his breath.

"You're human," he said. "You're allowed to fall apart sometimes."

I started to shake my head to argue the point, but I was tired. And, honestly, so off-kilter. "Okay," I whispered.

When his arms slid around my waist, and he held me for a few beats of my heart, all I could think was that no matter how unsettled I was, I truly did feel safe when I was with him.

The sound of the door opening onto the deck snapped through the moment. We stepped apart. My head whipped toward the noise, wondering who had come out. Someone shook a dustpan into the trash can tucked just outside the door on the porch.

"Are you still working?" Kincaid asked.

I took a shaky breath, gathering myself. "Yeah."

"I'll walk you back in."

A few minutes later, I was back in the rhythm. Although time and again, I found my gaze darting over to where Kincaid was at the bar with a few other firefighters.

Shelly was gone, and she'd left me a ridiculous tip. "You can't bribe me, Shelly," I whispered to the cash as I tucked it into my apron.

I knew I needed to talk to my mom about seeing her. I wasn't ready, though. I told myself I could deal with that on another day.

The heat from that brief kiss with Kincaid still felt like embers burning inside.

I fell asleep hours later at home, thoughts of him spinning through my mind.

# Chapter Eight

# KINCAID

"You got that?" I glanced over at my mom.

Her eyes twinkled as she replied, "Of course I've got it."

Her hand was curled around her cane, and it twisted my heart to see her using one. "Now, come on. Catch up, Kincaid," she teased.

A few minutes later, we were situated in an exam room at the doctor's office, and the friendly med assistant was smiling at my mom, who made light of absolutely everything when it came to her health.

My heart gave another twist when I looked over at her. The thing was, she was at peace. And yet, I constantly fended off worry on her behalf. She was all I had when it came to family for me. It had always been just me and her against the world.

It wasn't as if life with my mom had been perfect. There was no such thing. But there'd never been a moment where I doubted her love, and never a time when she didn't make the best of whatever the situation at hand offered us.

I was old enough now to know she had kept us going on a threadbare budget. She was a really good cook and made the best of what we had. To this day, one of my favorite comfort meals was whatever pasta she picked up at what I now knew was a food bank, tossed with nothing more than butter, chicken or beef, and whatever seasonings she had in the cabinet.

"How's your pain level?" Heidi, the med assistant, was asking.

My mom tilted her head to the side, lightly tapping her fingertips on one knee. "Well, I'd like to lie and tell you it's fine." She lifted one shoulder in barely a shrug. "I live with pain, but I hate pain medication. It makes my brain fuzzy."

Heidi nodded, her eyes flicking to mine briefly. "How about you rate your pain on a scale of one to ten?"

My mom rolled her eyes. "Heidi, get real with me."

Heidi smiled slightly, but her brow furrowed, and worry flickered in her eyes. "I know you're going to tell me you just live with it, but I'd like to know how bad it feels for you. Quality of life is important."

My mother's sigh filtered out. "Well, a ten is if I'm in the emergency room and something truly horrible has happened, say a bone is sticking out of my leg."

Heidi's eyes widened slightly while I snorted. "My mom definitely tries not to exaggerate," I offered dryly.

"So I'm going to go with…" My mother paused, tapping her fingers on the handle of her cane now. "Six or seven. Average."

"Mom," I muttered, running a hand through my hair.

"Oh, my son would like me to never be in pain," she said with a slight smile and a nod.

"And, that's what we'd all like," Heidi offered. "I see from your chart that you got all of your records from your last doctor sent over to us," she added.

My mom thumbed toward me. "He did. He's a good boy."

Heidi's brows hitched up. "Oh, well, that's nice."

"My son's not a standard man. He takes care of records, notes, appointments, and the like," my mom piped up.

I nodded. "She taught me how to do that. I do understand, in our world, that might not be the norm."

"Well, all credit to you, Claudia," Heidi offered with a brow waggle.

I chuckled. "That's where it should go."

"Back to your pain, you've pretty much tried everything we could offer from my review of your chart," Heidi said. "I'm sure you know most pain medications aren't good to use long-term. There are a few things we could do with physical therapy. Would you like to try that?"

"Please. It does help," my mother said.

"All right. I'll set up that referral." Heidi's gaze arced toward me. "I understand your son is a hotshot firefighter. So what's your plan for transportation when he's not available?"

"I'll figure it out. I'm very good at making friends." My mom's tone was firm and confident. She was the kind of person who made friends everywhere she went and still stayed in touch with people she'd met on trips.

Heidi laughed softly. "I'm sure you are. We'll get that referral set up. It usually takes a week or two after we make the referral before someone will call you to schedule. It'll come from one of the numbers for Willow Brook Hospital. If you have unknown callers silenced, maybe just put in their main number. That should make sure it comes through. Or you can always just wait for the message and call back."

"I can handle that," my mom said.

"No doubt," Heidi said, her gaze sobering for a beat. "So, Dr. Charlie's going to come in. She'll review everything. Thanks for getting your bloodwork taken care of ahead of time."

"Always. I don't love needles, but I'm used to them," my mom said with a dismissive wave.

"Anything else we should know about?" Heidi prompted.

"I'm doing as well as could be expected," my mother said, her chin lifting slightly.

"Fair enough."

After a moment, there was a light knock at the door while the med assistant was entering a few things into the laptop. "Here she is," Heidi said, gesturing toward the woman who entered. "Dr. Charlie."

My mom smiled up at her. "Hello, hello." She thrust a hand out.

Dr. Charlie and I had met at my mom's first appointment a few weeks ago. So far, I liked her. The doctor smiled, pushing her glasses up on her nose. "And, how are we today, Claudia?" Dr. Charlie asked.

"We are well, and you?"

"Same. I would say, after reviewing everything, things look copacetic."

"Ooh, I love that word," my mom enthused.

"Do you now?" the doctor teased lightly.

"It's a good word." My mom nodded firmly.

"We're going to make a referral for physical therapy to hopefully help with her pain. She doesn't like any of the pain medication options," Heidi chimed in.

Dr. Charlie cocked her head to the side, studying my mom before nodding. "Understood. Do you want something for those bad days?"

My mom shook her head. "No, thank you. If it's *that* bad, then I probably need more than pain medication. I just don't like how they make me feel all fuzzy and loopy."

"You're not the only one who says that. All right. So we'll make that referral for physical therapy." Dr. Charlie's gaze slid to mine. "Any questions? Concerns?"

"I don't think so."

"Is there anything I need to be monitoring more?" I asked. I felt more than saw my mother roll her eyes. She gave off a vibe when she did that, and it was strong.

"I don't think so. Your mother has her Lupus well monitored. I'm glad you're here to support her," Dr. Charlie replied.

"Of course you're glad he's here," my mom said. "He takes good care of me, but I take good care of him too."

"I've no doubt about that," Dr. Charlie said with a warm smile.

After we left, the car was quiet for a few minutes as I drove before my mom spoke. "You know this isn't terminal, Kincaid."

My chest felt tight, and I had to take a slow breath to help loosen it enough to speak. "I know. But you're not going to live forever, Mom."

"I know," she exclaimed. "But I'm also not going anywhere anytime soon, and no one lives forever. I'm only fifty-five, and Dr. Charlie agrees with my last doctor. I should have an average life expectancy."

I let out a sharp breath. "I just hate seeing you in pain, Mom."

She fell quiet for a few beats. "I know you do."

I reached over and squeezed her hand.

"In the meantime, stop treating me like I'm an invalid. I just have a cane," she ordered.

I released her hand, shaking my head as a laugh sputtered out. "I will endeavor not to treat you like an invalid."

"Oh, good vocabulary," she teased.

My mind spun back to when I was a little boy, when she used to help me with my homework. She became an English teacher after she left the Air Force, and she had high standards.

"So, speaking of me not living forever..." she began before a loaded pause. "When are you going to have me a grandchild?"

This time, my laugh was a startled choke. "Jesus, Mom. Give me some time."

"Well, chop, chop." She let out a little laugh. "Obviously, I'm teasing. It's fine if you don't want to have children. That said, I would hope you would be open to some kind of relationship."

Tori instantly strolled into my thoughts. In all honesty, she was the first woman I'd ever met where I thought maybe, *maybe*, I might want more than something superficial. And yet, the baggage around relationships was heavy for me. Largely thanks to the father I'd never met. He was a big part of the reason, or at least it felt like to me, that my mom had wanted to come back to

Alaska. She insisted that wasn't the driving force for her, but I wasn't so sure.

"If it ever feels right," I said slowly, "I might consider a relationship."

"Oh, my God. That is ridiculously vague," my mother pointed out.

"Says the woman who went through life insisting she didn't need anyone," I countered.

"Well, I didn't, and you don't either. Not like that. It's more than that. We all need each other, but it doesn't have to be romance." She paused. "Kincaid, you're a good man, and I want the best for you."

"I know, Mom. I know." I took a slow breath. "We'll see."

# Chapter Nine

# TORI

"Seriously, Mom?"

I slid a mug of coffee across the table to her. We were sitting in our usual corner at Firehouse Café. She lifted her hands and let them fall. "I understand that it's different for you than it is for me. I really do. But I hate to see that you're letting Shelly get to you. You could try to shift your thinking about it. That's what I've done. I'm not even talking about forgiveness. I'm talking about letting go."

"What's the difference?" I ignored the stinging burn in my heart whenever I thought about Shelly and my father and the aftermath of their betrayal. The rest of us in their orbit were nothing more than collateral damage, wreckage they left behind.

"Forgiveness is..." My mother took a quick breath, her gaze contemplative. "I guess, a blessing that you forgive them as a person for doing that. I don't really forgive Shelly. In a way—as you know—her actions in what happened hurt me more than your father's actions." She took a swallow of her coffee, rolling her eyes. "But as much as that's true, I had to let it go, or it would char my soul. At least, that's how it felt. I hope you can let it go."

I let out a sharp sigh and took a bite of my bagel, chewing

through my frustration. "I just can't believe she moved back," I said after a moment.

"Honey, her family's here," my mother pointed out gently.

"Yeah, and they suck."

My mother's eyes crinkled at the corners, slightly amused. She shrugged. "Shelly is living with the consequences of her choices. I've let it go. I honestly have no reaction when I see her. You forget that I *had* to find a way to be civil. Because you had to visit your father until you turned eighteen, so I had to find a way to make it not awful for me. I wouldn't say I let it go back then, but I accepted it. I had to. As for your father..." she shrugged. "Same goes for him. In the end, he regretted his choices because they destroyed his relationship with you."

My father had died a few years ago, young-ish, from a massive, unexpected coronary event. At the time, I remembered thinking it was because his heart was black. And yet, I also knew that I had to carry the weight of the bitterness that marred our relationship after everything went down. Sometimes, it felt like I had scorch marks in my heart. The ground felt barren and burned in places.

"I just can't get over Shelly's nerve," I finally said.

"Yeah, well, here's the thing. People do what they do. They hurt other people. They make mistakes. They don't think through their choices when they're in the midst of them."

"That's one way to put it," I commented, my tone dry as dust.

It still surprised me, but my mom really did seem to have let this whole thing go. Meanwhile, I wanted her to be as angry and bitter as I was. At the same time, she deserved the peace she had found, and I wanted her to have it. I knew it was earned, a bit of hard, sweet peace she'd had to fight for.

"Maybe you should hear her out," she finally added.

"What?" I sputtered, relieved I'd just finished chewing a bite because, otherwise, I would have choked.

"I did," my mom replied.

"You did?"

"Yes. Honestly, at first, when they were still together and when they moved to Anchorage, I had to live with the shame and the embarrassment, and so many feelings of being a failure as a woman. Letting go wasn't something I could do at that time. I won't lie. I said it to her, and I'll say it to anyone who asks. Yeah. When your father cheated on her too, and it all blew up, and she realized she wasn't special, that she'd fallen for some of the oldest bullshit in the book, I felt some satisfaction at that. But now, I don't even feel that. That was more, I guess, validating at the time. It helped me see that it wasn't something wrong with me. I didn't have a specific flaw. It was your father. I finally talked to Shelly." My brows practically hit my hairline, but my mother shrugged lightly. "Figured I might as well get it over with. When I heard her out, I was able to let go more. I think she'll always live with a lot of shame for what happened. It hurt all of us, including her."

All I could do was stare at my mother, my throat tight and tears burning hot in my eyes. The blast radius from the path of my father's and Shelly's choices left a debris field that remained.

"Shelly apologized. I do believe she meant it. She takes accountability, but she has to live with the fact that there's a certain amount of trust I can never extend to her. I absolutely understand you can't trust her again either." My mother's gaze was soft as she held mine. "But maybe you need to just hear her out, so you can find a path toward peace."

"You know what I hate the most?"

"What?"

"Aside from losing everything I believed about my father, because that sucked," I said flatly. I took a quick breath. "I just don't trust. Not in relationships. There's always a question mark. Because I never, *never*, believed Dad could do what he did, but he did."

"I know, sweetheart," my mom said softly. "But trust is worth it. I promise you. I have other friendships, and I have complete faith in them. Not everybody will hurt you. It's just not true."

I blinked away the tears stinging my eyes. My mind spun to that moment the other night when I kissed Kincaid. I felt so safe with him in that moment. *That* was terrifying for me.

I didn't feel safe with men. *Ever.* Letting down my guard wasn't something I could imagine doing. And yet, somehow, I had. With him. That was so shocking to me.

Just then, the bell chimed on the door at the café. I reflexively glanced over to see the man in question walking in. He was with Leo Massie, another firefighter in town. The mere sight of Kincaid set my pulse off like the buzzer at the start of a race. My cheeks heated, and my belly swooped in a dizzying spin just as his eyes locked with mine.

I tore my eyes away from Kincaid's, promptly running straight into my mother's gaze. Her lips twitched at the corners as a teasing glint entered her eyes. "Well, who might that be?"

I cleared my throat. "Nobody," I squeaked.

My mother's chuckle was low. "Well, he looks like he knows you, so..."

"Oh, my God," I hissed under my breath. "Mom!"

"Obviously, he's a firefighter. There are firefighters aplenty around here," my mom said with a shrug.

"He's the firefighter who stopped to help me when I had the bee sting situation," I said under my breath.

"He took you to the hospital, right?" my mother clarified.

"Yes."

"Well, he's a good man, then."

I thought about my father and about all the good things he had done when he was a police officer in Willow Brook. He had been beloved around town. As a result, when the whole truth came out, many people had been shocked.

"Dad was a good man too, Mom. Or, so I thought."

She paused, sadness flickering in her eyes. "Nobody is all one thing."

"What do you mean?"

"Just that. It isn't black and white when it comes to anyone. Obviously, I was very hurt by what happened with your father, and it took me a long time to reach this point. But I do recognize that he was the man who was so beloved in the community. He was a good father. And, he was also the man who made a choice that was very hurtful for you and for me."

My throat felt tight, aching with that old blockage of emotion I never knew what to do with. I took a shaky breath. "Mom," I began.

She shook her head sharply. "You know it's true. Obviously, I have no idea what Kincaid is like in all facets, but he stopped and helped you. He didn't have to."

"He's a firefighter," I pointed out.

"Well, sure, but if memory serves, he wasn't on duty. He heard sweet Bella barking, and that's why he came over to help you."

I'd filled my mom in on the details of that afternoon when she took me to the mechanic to pick up my car after they repaired the bent rim the following day. I cleared my throat, breathing slowly and trying to ease the tightness and achiness that had taken up residence in my heart so many years ago. Back when I truly grappled with the depth of my father's betrayal.

"I know," I finally said.

My mom paused, her brows hitching up slightly before she added, "Clearly, you think Kincaid is handsome."

"Well, I mean objectively speaking, he is." I ignored the heat climbing up my neck into my cheeks.

My mother's laugh was dry as she shook her head slightly. "Yes, I'm sure it's just objective. But you don't usually blush when—" she gestured subtly toward Levi Phillips, another firefighter I knew, who happened to be standing at the counter.

I'd been a few years behind Levi in high school. He was a huge flirt and friendly with everyone. "I know Levi's handsome," I said with a shrug, striving to come off as casual.

"And yet, I don't see that kind of reaction toward him."

"Mom," I ground out.

Her eyes twinkled just as Casey stopped beside our table, a tray balanced on her arm. "Should I get those plates?"

I nodded. "Go for it. My scone was delicious."

"Luna is such a good baker," Casey replied.

"The baked goods here have always been good," my mother added.

Janet happened to overhear as she was passing by. She stopped beside us, smiling warmly at my mom. "I appreciate your loyalty, but Luna's baked goods are absolutely better than mine."

My mom chuckled as she shrugged. "If you say so, Janet."

Janet's hand fell to my mom's shoulder and she gave her a gentle squeeze. "I do say so. How are you two doing, by the way?"

"We're good. I'm just so glad to have my daughter back in town full-time now."

"We all are," Janet said softly.

I knew Janet knew all the drama around my dad's affair with Shelly. I guess I'd just blocked out how much I'd hated it and how it affected me. Sometimes, forgetting didn't work.

Casey collected our plates and spun away to another table, while Janet and my mother fell into a conversation about mundane things, the kind of calm, easy talk you could only have with people who had seen you through hell and back. I sat there, gathering myself inside, reminding myself that the whole mess was in the past. *So* far in the past. It was all for the best. It didn't matter that Shelly was here in town again. It didn't matter that I didn't believe in love or didn't really trust anyone.

It didn't matter that Kincaid had kissed me and made me feel safe and made me want things I never thought I'd even want. None of that mattered, right?

# Chapter Ten

# TORI

After finishing up a lunch shift at Fireweed Winery, I was walking out to my car in the back lot when I heard, "Tori?"

Even though I told myself I wasn't positive that voice belonged to Kincaid, my nervous system sure thought it was him. A frisson of electricity danced over my skin as I turned and saw him approaching, his boots crunching on the gravel.

I stopped, my pulse taking off at a mad gallop. "Hi!" I squeaked.

*Seriously? You can speak like a normal human. He's just a man. Who cares if he kissed you?*

But when he stopped in front of me, and his eyes, warm and cognac-hued, locked with mine, I felt all tingly inside and my belly shimmied.

"How's it going?" he asked easily, his tone calm and level.

"Fine." Still squeaky. Fuck my life. I couldn't even talk like a regular person. I rallied and attempted a normal conversation. "Just finishing up work. What are you doing here?"

Still squeaky. It wasn't quite as bad as if I had inhaled helium from a balloon, but I felt silly. I could feel the heat burning up my cheeks.

"Picking up takeout." He paused, glancing over his shoulder

at the sound of a vehicle backing up. "I have a question," he added when he turned back.

"Ask away!" I exclaimed, a little too forcefully, but hey, finally not squeaky. For the win.

"We have a fundraiser for the fire station, and uh, I need a date."

"You need a date?" I parroted back to him because my conversational skills were awesome.

"Yeah, that's what I just said."

"Oh, um, okay. Are you looking for recommendations on who you should bring?" I asked next, as if that made *any* sense at all.

His eyes crinkled a little at the corners, his lips twitching slightly. "Well, I was wondering if you would go with me."

"Me?" My hand flew to my chest, rather dramatically, as if we were in a soap opera.

"Yes, *you*, Tori," he said, that hint of a smile unfurling across his face.

My belly went from a swoop to a full-on gymnastics routine. My hormones? They were doing cheerleading stunts. "Oh." Holy wow, one word.

"What do you think?" he prompted, oblivious to my internal state.

Oh, my God, this was so embarrassing. I could not behave like a normal human being. "People don't usually ask me out on dates," I finally said.

"Well," he replied with a grin, "*I'm* asking you out on a date."

"Oh," I repeated. "Are you sure you want me to go with you?"

Kincaid tipped his head to the side, studying me quietly. I felt completely unsettled under his attention. There was a rustle of wind in the trees nearby. The lights from the back of the winery illuminated a few loose leaves drifting to the ground. I didn't know how to handle his calm regard and the inquisitiveness in his gaze. It felt as if he could see right into my heart. Somehow, he reached inside and held it carefully for me.

"I'm sure about that, Tori," he finally said, his tone low and clear.

"Okay," I said. Again, my voice was too forceful, but not squeaky.

"Does that mean yes?" he clarified, his eyes warm.

I nodded vigorously. "That means yes."

"Do you need to know when it is?" he prompted.

"Oh, there's always that," I said, suddenly sheepish. "When?"

"It's actually this weekend, on Saturday." He paused, just a flicker of hesitation in him. The first one I'd seen. "I hadn't been planning on bringing anyone, and then they asked if any of us without dates would be part of an auction, and I'd rather not do that. But more than that..." He shrugged. "After we kissed, well, I'd like to take you out."

I swallowed through the anxiety spinning in my chest. "Okay, um, okay." For fuck's sake, I needed to pull it together. "Is it a fancy event? Casual? What is it, and where is it?"

"Apparently, they rented the event room here. Seeing as this is Alaska, I think casual is probably fine. They didn't really give us a dress code."

"Okay, okay. I'll figure something out."

"Okay," he repeated with a bemused smile.

I started to back away, my bag slung over my shoulder, but Kincaid reached out, catching my hand in his. His touch was like a jolt of lightning sizzling up my arm, spinning through me, and lighting every nerve ending on fire.

"What is it?" I asked.

He gave the slightest pressure to my hand, as if giving me space to pull away. I didn't want to. Instead, I stepped closer, because that's what almost everything in me—everything except the tightly-wound distrust coiled in my chest—wanted.

"Just this," he said softly, before dipping his head and brushing his lips over mine.

His touch was soft, but electric. I actually sighed when he pulled back, a sharp sense of loss filling the space between us.

I wanted more. I wanted to plaster myself against him. To climb him like a tree. To get utterly lost in another kiss like the one from the other night. The heat in his eyes felt like a promise.

He thumbed over his shoulder. "We have an audience."

I glanced over to see a tourist bus had rolled into the parking lot with a group already disembarking. "Oh." I let out a breathless, startled laugh.

"So, I'll text you?" he prompted.

"What time is it?" I asked.

He blinked. "Oh, you mean what time is the fundraiser. Right." He gave a little head shake, and I thought maybe he was a little discombobulated too. "Six o'clock. Are you working?"

I shook my head, relieved for once that my shift wasn't scheduled that night. "Nope."

"I'll see you then."

A moment later, I watched him walk toward his truck. I climbed into my car and sat there for a minute before I lifted my fingers to my lips. They were still tingling.

I took a shaky breath and whispered to myself, "See you then."

# Chapter Eleven

# KINCAID

"You're bringing Tori?" Maisie sputtered, her eyes widening slightly.

"Yeah, is that a problem?"

Maisie blinked a few times. "No."

I chuckled because she looked so startled. "Well, you told me we could bring dates, so, I have a date."

"You have a date?" a voice came from behind me.

I glanced over, catching Griffin's gaze. "Yeah. Is that a problem with you?"

Beck joined the conversation as he came through the doorway. "It is a problem for no one. Tori's good people."

"Good people?" Griffin arched a brow.

"She grew up here. She was a few years behind me in school," Beck explained.

"Cade knows her well," Beck added as Cade Masters came walking in from the police station side of the building and rested his elbows on the counter.

"Who do I know well?" Cade asked, his gaze bouncing between us.

"Tori Shackelford," Beck added.

"Ah, yeah, Tori's great," Cade said simply.

"How do you know her so well?" I asked, a little too casually.

Cade's brows hitched slightly. "Her dad worked with mine on the police force here for years. Left after the drama."

"Drama?" Maisie prompted quickly.

Griffin glanced at her, waggling his brows. "Holy smokes, is there town gossip that Maisie doesn't know?"

"Hey," Maisie said, narrowing her eyes. "I'm the main dispatcher. I hear all the news. What do you mean, drama?" Her gaze whipped between Beck and Cade.

"Babe, this is old news. It was years before you moved here," Beck said. "I'd just graduated from high school."

"To make a long story short," Cade jumped in, "Tori's dad was on the police force, and everybody loved him. My dad loved him. Hell, I loved him. My mom used to babysit Tori plenty. Everything blew up because her dad was having an affair with Tori's mom's best friend. They were so close that Tori called her 'Aunt Shelly.' That gossip all but burned the phone lines in town."

Oh. *This* was the history Tori had told me about. I guess I hadn't realized the scale of the fallout. I hadn't contemplated how it would've rippled through a town this size.

Cade shook his head. "It was ugly. Up until then, Tori's dad was beloved."

"Like yours," Beck offered.

"Something like that," Cade replied. "Anyway, Tori's dad and Shelly split town. Even got married."

Maisie's mouth dropped open before she closed it, her eyes snapping. "Oh, I don't like this story at all."

"It's not a story. It's what happened," Cade said dryly. "Anyway, Tori's mom never left town. Her dad and Shelly moved to Anchorage. I don't even know how things went for them. I know my mom felt really bad. She and Tori's mom were pretty close. Still are."

"Shit happens, you know," Beck added with a sigh. "I guess you never know what some people will do."

I thought about Tori crying the other night, the emotion in

her voice, and the bruised vulnerability she carried like armor. I wanted to find her dad and clock him one. Not because she needed me to, but damn, that was shitty.

"Wow. Talk about trust issues," Maisie said.

Quiet fell around us for a few beats.

"People do shitty things," Griffin muttered.

"Is her dad still around?" I couldn't help but ask.

Cade shook his head. "Nah. Passed away from a heart attack, I think. Shelly just moved back to town."

Maisie's eyes narrowed, anger all but coming off of her in sparks. Considering that I was furious at Tori's dad and Shelly, I understood the feeling. I wanted to fix everything for Tori.

"Well, fuck," Griffin finally said. "That's a depressing story."

"Nobody's perfect," Beck commented.

"Well, there's nobody's perfect, and then there's brutal betrayal on multiple levels. You better be nice to Tori," Maisie added, her gaze swinging to me.

I held up both my hands. "Hey, I haven't done anything. I'm definitely not planning to marry her, or anyone else for that matter, and have a decade-long affair with someone's best friend. Sheesh," I muttered under my breath.

Beck clapped me on the shoulder. "Good. Don't be an ass. Loyalty matters, you know."

I thought of my own father, who hadn't even bothered to stick around at all. I knew well how much it mattered, and what it meant when someone couldn't even be bothered. "I know," was all I said.

———

The afternoon before the fundraiser, my mom's physical therapist was coming over. My mom adored him.

"Chris is the best," she said when she heard the doorbell ring.

"All I want is for you to be in less pain," I replied, meaning it completely.

I wasn't ready to say it out loud, and I almost hesitated to even think it, but my mom did seem to be getting stronger. She had actually gone up and down the small set of entrance stairs several times without her cane. Although I had purposefully bought a single-story home, there were two areas where there were three steps leading from one area to another, along with the steps in the front.

"Hey, Chris," I called over as he walked in.

He flashed a grin. "Hey, hey. Your mom's doing great."

"I know. She seems to be."

My mom just beamed at him. Chris chuckled and immediately got to work on the latest routine of exercises for her.

"Kincaid has a date," my mother announced as he was stretching one of her knees.

Chris winked when he looked my way. "I heard about it."

"You heard about my date?" I sputtered in disbelief.

"Dude, have you lived in small-town Alaska before?"

"There are small towns everywhere, and gossip is always a thing," I countered. "I guess I just didn't expect my mom's physical therapist to be privy to my dating life."

"For better or worse, gossip runs hot in Alaska, because we're so far from everything. Local news *is* the news."

"It's for the fundraiser," I felt the need to point out.

"Her name is Tori Shackelford," my mother added.

"Mom. How do you even know her name?" I managed to keep from sighing in frustration.

"I have my sources," she said, lifting her chin slightly and looking a little haughty.

I bit back a laugh. "You're the collector of gossip."

"About you," she said unabashedly.

"Where did you hear this?" I couldn't help but ask Chris.

"Well, apparently some of your fellow firefighters told Nate about it, because he's going with Holly. Obviously, I work with Holly at the hospital since I'm a nurse and a physical therapist. All this to say, that's how I have the scoop." He waggled his brows. "Holly and Tori are old friends. I knew Tori growing up. She's always been a great person. You'd better be good to her."

"I'm getting the impression that no matter what I do, I better not fuck it up," I muttered.

My mom tugged on the hem of Chris's T-shirt, and his attention shifted to her. She smiled up at him. "Kincaid is a good man. He would never hurt anyone."

Chris held her gaze for a long beat and nodded slowly. "And, you're a good mom."

She lifted one shoulder in a tiny, dismissive shrug. "Maybe. I tried."

"Well, you told me you were a single mom. That means, you alone are largely responsible for being the role model your son needed to turn into a good man," Chris pointed out.

My mom beamed again. Having my mom's love and pride was a gift I would never dismiss. I knew I was lucky in that regard.

After Chris got focused on his session with my mom, I headed outside to take care of a few things around the yard. I hadn't found much time yet to take care of spring yard cleaning. The air still carried a bite to it even though it was almost May, but when the sun hit just right, you could believe warmer days were coming. As I clipped a few dead limbs from the trees near the house, my thoughts kept spinning back to Tori. Of course, thoughts of Tori lead straight to the way her lips had felt against mine.

I was halfway up the steps to the deck a little while later, just brushing the dirt from my palms, when Chris stepped out. The door clicked shut behind him, and he paused, looking over at me with that easy smile of his. "Your mom really is doing well," he said.

"I'm hoping so." I paused, my chest tightening just a little. "Sometimes I can't tell." My heart twisted.

When one person is the only constant in your world—the only real family you can count on—the world can start to feel really small. My mom's parents had been there for us when I was little, but they'd both passed within the last ten years. No drama to it. Just life. The slow wear and tear of time, and eventually, their bodies gave out. It was that ordinary kind of loss, and yet it left a hole.

I didn't like contemplating a world without my mom in it. She was a touchstone for me and had always been. I couldn't imagine anyone else taking her place in that role. Ever.

"Thanks for taking such good care of her, by the way. She enjoys working with you," I added.

Chris's smile widened, and the warmth behind it hit me in the chest. "She's easy," he said. Then, after a pause, he added more seriously, "You know she's going to be okay, right?"

I paused as my heart stuttered for a beat. The truth was, I didn't know. Not really. I hated how much my fear was interfering with what I knew rationally. "I mean... I'm hoping so."

Chris gave a small nod. "I mean it. She is okay. I know you know this, but it bears repeating. Lupus is a chronic condition. She's going to experience flare-ups. But she's strong, otherwise. Her heart and lungs are in great shape." He glanced toward the house for a second before continuing. "She had a rough patch, yeah. But things have stabilized again. Honestly? I think menopause threw her off worse than the condition itself. A lot of people don't talk about that part."

I blinked. "Menopause?"

Chris nodded. "Yup. Doesn't get nearly enough airtime with medical professionals, in my opinion. Women don't even need an underlying condition to get knocked sideways by it. Your mom has had both going on at once. That's a tough combination. She's getting stronger every week. I can see it."

His phone vibrated in his pocket, and he pulled it out, checking the screen. "Gotta roll," he said. He took a few steps down the stairs before turning back with a grin. "Have fun on your date."

I watched his car disappear down the driveway. An eagle called nearby, the sound sharp. The wind gusted with a swirl, spinning some dead leaves on the gravel drive. The moment I stepped through the front door, I knew I was in trouble.

My mom was already holding two shirts in front of her, both of which looked like they hadn't seen the light of day in months. Her expression was all too familiar, which meant opinions were incoming.

"You're not wearing that shirt from the other night," she said, giving me a once-over, her gaze sharp. "You are going to this fundraiser with a date. You need to wear something that looks nice."

I groaned. "So help me God..."

# Chapter Twelve

# TORI

It was kind of odd to be a customer at the place where I worked. Not because anyone made it feel that way, but it just felt strange to sit in a space where I was usually carrying trays, delivering food and drinks, and the like. My muscle memory kept wanting to jump in and help. Tish was firmly holding me at bay and handling hosting duties tonight.

"It's our contribution," she said, narrowing her eyes at me as if I were about to snatch a tray and start bussing tables. "But our contribution does *not* include one of our waitstaff who is here for social reasons, trying to sneak in unpaid labor." She swatted me away just as Griffin stopped beside her and slid an arm around her waist.

"The food is amazing," he said, patting his stomach.

Tish flushed a little, smiling. "Thank you. I'll give your compliments to the chef."

"It's David," Griffin said with a little chuckle.

David was the longtime chef from the original Fireweed Winery location in Fireweed Harbor. He'd insisted on coming out here when they opened this expansion restaurant, even though he was supposed to be trying to slow down his work schedule these days. He still handled the menu and managed things, but they were definitely in the market for someone to take on the full-time role.

"He's working more than I would like," Tish chimed in with a frown. "If you know anyone, let us know."

"I'll ask around," I offered. "I've got a few friends in Anchorage who work in the restaurant scene."

Tish got pulled away into a conversation with some arriving guests. Meanwhile, Kincaid and I wandered over to stand near one of the cocktail tables lining the edges of the room. The silent auction for artwork was in full swing now, with bidding moving along at a good clip. All of the works were from Alaskan artists, which made the event even more special.

One of those artists, Jasmine, stopped beside us. She was glowing with her hair spun in a loose knot and her smile warm and bright.

"Tori, I keep meaning to find you when you're not working," she said.

"Well, good news," I replied, gesturing to my skirt paired with a silk blouse and heels. "I'm officially off the clock."

"You two know each other, I presume?" Kincaid asked, amusement lacing in his voice.

Jasmine grinned, just as her husband Donovan, also a firefighter, strolled over and rested a hand on her shoulder.

"Good to see you. Are you up to speed yet?" Donovan said to Kincaid, eyes crinkling with a smile.

"Up to speed?" Jasmine asked, peering up at him.

"Getting to know everyone here," he said. "Small-town living's a whole different beast when it's new. It's like everyone else went to the same school, has the same stories, and you're just trying to figure out who all the characters are."

"Jasmine was a few years ahead of me in school," I added. "So we didn't overlap too much when we were younger."

She shrugged. "I'm just glad you're back. Speaking of, have you come to card night yet?" she asked.

I blinked. "Um, when is it next?"

Before she could answer, Luna and Casey appeared, each with drinks in hand.

"Even *I* know when card night is," Casey said, nudging my arm. "Tori, you have to come."

"I do?"

"Yes," Casey said with a firm nod.

For a flash, a lingering and familiar uncertainty flickered inside. I'd been in high school when my family's drama exploded. It had deeply affected me, in the sense of feeling like I wanted to hide from everyone. I couldn't help but remember those moments when I was just trying to find my place in the midst of the mess. I'd felt as if I was always on the outer edges of things, just trying to keep my head low and out of anyone's attention. As a result, I mostly avoided social events.

It hadn't helped that my former friend—Shelly's daughter—had been one of the more popular girls. She developed a talent for sweet exclusion, always managing to make it clear I wasn't quite welcome.

When the gossip exploded all those years ago, I remember feeling as if I were a piñata. The one being smacked over and over in someone else's celebration—bits of my life flying everywhere while people gathered to collect whatever pieces they could and gossip about them later.

None of it felt good, no matter how juicy and saccharine sweet the gossip about my family had been. Now, with everyone smiling and chatting all around, I felt unsettled and uncertain. Maybe it was just me trying to find my footing in a place that was once home, that I'd left feeling cast out.

Tonight, I was on a date—with Kincaid. Someone who made me feel like I wasn't a piñata anymore. That maybe I could start anew, blaze a fresh trail in my life.

"It's at Lucy and Levi's place," Jasmine was saying. "He has a new hamster."

"A hamster?" A laugh sputtered out of me.

"I know, right? My husband has a pet hamster. He had one

named Ham for years," Lucy chimed in, appearing at Jasmine's side with a bemused grin.

"Out of curiosity, how long do hamsters live?" Jasmine asked.

"About three years," Lucy replied. "So, yeah, Ham passed. There was even a funeral."

Kincaid carefully schooled his expression to neutral. "A funeral for a pet hamster?" he asked.

Lucy was tiny, almost fairy-like, with her long blond hair and petite size. I glanced between her and Jasmine and back to Kincaid. Lucy shrugged. "Yup, for a hamster. Anyway, please come," she added. "We're working on letting the new hamster run loose in the house. Ham was unusual in that regard. Tomorrow night, around six?"

"Should I pick you up?" Casey asked, looking at me hopefully.

Before I knew it, I was nodding. Apparently, I had plans tomorrow evening. The rest of the night rolled along, and I was acutely aware of Kincaid's presence the entire time. I tried to remember the last time I went on a date, and I was pretty sure it had been in college. Which was kind of ironic, considering how much of a bust college had been for me. I'd never been able to figure out what I wanted to do. I'd drifted from major to major before graduating.

Despite that aimlessness, since I'd moved back home to Willow Brook, I felt like I was settling into something more solid. A position with Fireweed Industries was coming together, possibly an events coordinator role I hadn't expected to want, but actually did. In the meantime, I genuinely liked waitressing. I loved talking to people. I liked the rhythm of it, the motion, the bustle, the conversations. My shifts flew by.

But dating? That hadn't flown at all, much less ever gotten off the ground. I'd dated a bit in college. Nothing serious and nothing that lasted. I hadn't dated at all in high school—mostly out of sheer embarrassment about the scandal that had blown up around my dad and the sharp edge of anger about all of it that pricked under my skin.

I'd tried to shove that anger down in college, but it never went away. I'd never been surprised that none of my dating relationships went anywhere. I didn't trust, at all. I'd never gone on a date with someone like Kincaid. He felt steady, grounded, and even kind. A man who made me feel like I didn't have to be anyone but myself, and that, somehow, was the most terrifying part.

"Shall we?" he said at one point, as the crowd started to thin out later in the evening.

"Shall we what?" I asked, confused.

He tipped his head slightly, his lips barely quirking at the corners. Just that hint of a smile sent sparks scattering like pinwheels across my skin. The low hum of my pulse revved louder.

"Shall we, you know, leave?" he asked.

"Have you done your duty?" I teased.

He looked around, scanning the room. "I think so. About half my crew left. We're in the clear."

We started to make our way out, and I felt his palm rest just above the curve of my lower back. The heat of it felt comforting as he gently coaxed me forward through the room.

The moment we stepped outside, the cool evening air struck my cheeks.

"Thank you," I said when we paused near the gravel parking lot.

"For what?" he asked.

"For taking me. That was nice."

This time, his smile stretched slowly from one corner of his mouth to the other—and my belly did a full swoop.

"Well, thank *you* for coming with me," he said.

I felt giddy as I smiled back at him. Our footsteps crunched over gravel as we resumed walking. I loved this time of year. It felt like the world was waking up again, coming alive after the deep hush of winter as spring began to take hold.

There were jokes galore about spring and mud season in Alaska and the blink of fall, but every season was distinct here and had its own charms. The days were getting longer, and even though it was fairly late in the evening, there were still remnants of light outside as the night came to gradually claim the sky from the day. The blue was fading into a soft, deep smudgy purple with the moon rising and the last glimmers of the sun shimmering above the mountain ridge in the distance.

In this moment, standing here with Kincaid, I didn't feel like I was carrying the weight of all my baggage. I just felt like a woman on a date, with a good man.

We stopped beside his truck, and all of my senses felt alive, tingling and attuned to him. An owl called somewhere nearby, its low hoot echoing in the quiet, followed by another answer farther off in the distance. A bird flew overhead, and the soft whoosh of its wings sliced through the night air.

"The woo-woo birds," I murmured, barely above a whisper.

"The woo-woo birds?" Kincaid asked, amusement glinting in his eyes.

"Yeah," I said, smiling faintly. "Their wings make that whistling sound. It's called winnowing. They're Wilson's snipes, small, fast birds that fly low. You can't always see them, but you can hear them. Woo-woo." I mimicked the sound, soft and airy.

"There's nothing amazing about how they look," I added, "but I love the sound."

He nodded slowly, his eyes never leaving mine. We'd stopped on the passenger side of his truck, and his hand was curled loosely around the handle. I tilted my head up, abruptly aware of how close we were, how still he was.

He lifted his free hand and gently brushed a strand of hair away from my forehead, his fingers grazing my skin. His feather-light touch along the outer shell of my ear sent a shiver skating down my spine. Goosebumps rose on my arms, and my breath caught.

An impulse struck me, fast and sudden. I leaned forward and pressed my lips into the small dip at the base of his throat. That warm little hollow—exposed beneath the open edge of his shirt—was too tempting. His skin was sun-kissed even now, in spring. But he lived a life outdoors, and it showed. I lingered there for a moment before pulling back. My knees felt unsteady, and my heart was racing.

His eyes—*God*, his eyes—were molten. "Tori," he rasped.

"Yeah?" I whispered. My voice was barely there. The world blurred around the edges, my thoughts hazy like fog.

"This," he murmured.

On the heels of a breath, his lips were on mine. I felt the shape of that word—*this*—as surely as I felt his mouth move against mine. It was all fire and heat and slow hunger. There were kisses, and then there were Kincaid's kisses.

He kissed away the doubts clanging in my thoughts. He kissed open the quiet in my heart that I didn't let anyone near. Even if fleeting, he made me forget the ache of old wounds.

I leaned into our kiss, into him, with everything I didn't know I was holding back. For a few weightless, shimmering moments, nothing else mattered but this. Every motion was slow, languid, teasing, and designed to bring me to my knees. My knees actually did give out, but, blessedly, I sagged against the truck behind me just as one of his arms banded around my waist to hold me close. I tried to breathe.

Kincaid drew back, dusting one kiss at one corner of my mouth and then the other before he claimed my lips again. This time, his tongue swept in, with not even an ounce of hesitation, and I loved it. I loved the way he just dove in. I loved the way I was burning up with need as I flexed against him.

All of him was strong and hard. I could feel the flex of the muscles in his arms, his strong, muscled chest. He gentled our kiss, lifting his head, whispering my name again. It took an effort to drag my eyes open. My breath was coming in shallow gasps as I stared up at him.

"We should go," he rasped.

Just then, I heard the sound of tires on gravel and the back door to the restaurant opening and closing. Voices spilled out into the parking lot before muting again.

"Oh," I said because that was all I could manage.

"Let me take you home."

"Okay." Wow. Two whole syllables that time.

He stepped back, and my mind was like static. My body was on fire, alight with heat and sparks flickering inside. When he opened the door and helped me into his truck, my knees were so wobbly that my foot slipped on the running board. He caught me by the hip. Even in that clumsy moment, with the press of his fingers holding me steady, felt like kindling on the fire burning inside.

# Chapter Thirteen

# KINCAID

The space in my truck felt loaded, weighted with a charge. The fuse of chemistry burning between us had been lit the moment we left the fundraiser, and the flame was racing fast.

Tori. It was that simple.

When we pulled up to her place, I asked, "Can I walk you up?"

She nodded, and I followed her to the steps. Just as we reached the door, a soft bark came from inside.

"Oh, I have to let Bella out," she said quickly.

"Of course."

Her sweet dog came out, circling Tori with obvious joy before circling me and giving me a sniff of approval.

"Nothing like the love of a dog," I said dryly.

Tori's smile was wide as she looked up at me while walking alongside Bella by the edge of the trees. "She's my best friend. Have you ever had a dog?" she asked.

I nodded. "I have. Growing up, but haven't had one since then. But I think about getting another one," I added.

"Well..." Her tone turned teasing. "You'd better watch out for Tiffany, then."

"Tiffany?" I echoed, raising a brow.

"She's married to Wes. She's the office manager at the vet clinic, and she's always trying to get me to adopt another dog."

"She sounds persistent." I chuckled.

"She is," Tori laughed. "Wes's mom runs the animal shelter, and between them, they're always looking for homes for rescues."

"Ah, I know Tiffany. Wes is a good guy."

"Yeah. Tiffany even tried to get me to take a cat once."

"Peaches is our station cat," I commented.

"I'm all for pets," Tori said.

"Oh, same. I love animals," I admitted. "But I'm a hotshot firefighter. When I'm gone for the summer, that's a long stretch."

"I'll take care of any pet you get when you're gone," she offered.

"Really?" I turned toward her.

"Of course. That's an easy yes."

"I didn't even ask," I pointed out.

"No," she said, grinning. "But I'm offering. Hypothetically, if you did ask, the answer would be yes."

After Bella did her business, she immediately trotted back up the stairs and onto the small porch. When Tori gestured for me to come in, I didn't hesitate. I didn't want the night to end. Not just yet.

As I stepped inside, my mind flicked, just briefly, to everyone who had warned me to be good to Tori. As if I'd be anything else. Still, it struck me, standing there in her quiet space, how different this felt. How much more than I could've ever expected. Even though we'd only had two kisses, it already felt like more.

Bella curled up on a dog bed in the living room, directly in front of a small wood stove.

"She likes the heat," Tori said with a smile, shrugging off her jacket.

"Well, of course she does. It's warm. Even though it's technically spring..." I glanced at the frost along the edge of the window. "It's still Alaska."

Tori hung her jacket on the hook by the door and turned to face me. Several beats passed in silence. A long pause stretched between us, brimming with everything unspoken and the embers of need burning low.

"Should I go?" I asked quietly.

"I don't want you to," she said, her cheeks flushing as she spoke.

"I don't want to leave," I added, my voice low in the quiet.

A soft snore from Bella floated through the room, and Tori's smile turned sheepish. "She snores."

I simply nodded. With a quiet motion, she bent to remove her boots. When she straightened, she took a step closer, her hands lifting to my shoulders. Her fingers curled lightly as she eased my jacket down, brushing it down my arms. I shrugged out of it, hanging it beside hers before turning back to face her.

"Here's the thing," I said, reaching for one of her hands.

Somehow, just touching her quieted the usual doubts that ricocheted around my brain. "I like you."

Tori blinked up at me, then cleared her throat. "That's handy," she said softly. "I like you too."

My lips curved into a smile. There was an intimacy building between us—something bracing and electric that made me feel alive in a way I hadn't in years. Instead of thinking too hard, I stepped closer. I let go of her hand and raised mine to lightly palm her cheek.

"I'm going to kiss you again," I whispered against her lips.

I loved that I could feel the curve of her smile when she murmured, "Please do."

I let myself savor the moment—the soft give of her lips underneath mine, the sweet taste of her, the way she sighed into the kiss like she was giving in to gravity. She arched against me, her tongue dancing with mine, her body all curves and strength.

When we broke apart, my restraint was a paper-thin wall

holding back a flood. Lust frayed the edges, demanding more. I scrambled for purchase inside.

Not because I didn't want her, but because I did. Too much, too fast, and I didn't want to fuck it up. This wasn't something I usually thought too hard about. And yet, tangled somewhere deep in me were the faded scars of absence, of growing up without a father. Of watching my mother carry it all alone. I didn't want to be that man to anyone.

I was scrambling to find my balance here. It wasn't that I'd never felt pure, hot want before. It was that this didn't just feel like lust. It felt like a riptide, and I was caught in its rush and force.

Tori's eyes were wide and her pupils dark. Her lips were kiss-swollen and her cheeks flushed. I opened my mouth to say something—hell if I knew what—when her palm pressed lightly to my chest.

"Are you about to tell me we should slow down?" she asked.

Her voice, low, raspy, and frayed with heat, cracked through me like lightning across a summer sky.

I let out a shaky laugh, answering honestly. "I don't know what I was about to say."

For the first time, uncertainty flickered in her eyes. She blinked up at me before lifting her chin, almost defensively.

"Why did you ask that?" I prompted gently.

Her teeth lightly caught her bottom lip, and I was abruptly aware of the swollen, hard length of my cock. "I'm not sure. All I know is I don't want to stop."

Only Tori had this effect on me. Every time I thought maybe I had my balance with her, she kicked my feet out from under me. It was a kind of chaos, and yet it felt so fucking good. "I don't want to stop," I said honestly.

"Good." I could feel the heat of her palm just over my heart as its beat raced along.

"I don't want you to think this is just about sex," I added.

Uncertainty flickered in her eyes again, and I felt the sting of her pain on my own heart. "What do you mean?"

"Exactly that. I like you, Tori."

Tori's hand twisted a little bit on my chest, and she shifted on her feet. She was quiet for several long beats before she nodded. "I like you." She cleared her throat. "And it's not just about sex. Not for me."

Her palm stretched open across my heart again, sliding up, her fingers dipping into the very spot where she had dropped a kiss earlier. Everywhere she touched felt like flames on my skin. Her hand slid up further, curling around my nape and tugging me down slightly.

It was the easiest thing in the world to tumble into another kiss, to claim her mouth again, to savor the way she felt. The kiss once again started slow, yet it rapidly escalated. Our teeth clanked. It was messy and wild until we broke apart once again, the sound of our breath heaving in the air around us. We were plastered together. The evidence of my arousal pressed just above the cradle of Tori's hips. She swallowed before glancing over her shoulder. I followed her gaze to see that Bella was still sound asleep, still snoring.

"Come here," she said, stepping away and catching one of my hands in hers.

Alaska was filled with small houses like Tori's. Her entrance led into an open living room, kitchen, and dining area with a tall, peaked ceiling. There was a small balcony railing up above, and she led me over to the stairs that were off to one side. With every step I took, I could feel the drumbeat of my heart thumping faster and faster, picking up its pace. We crested the top of the stairs, which had a small open area with some bookshelves and a pair of chairs.

Although it was mostly dark out, I could see that the view would be beautiful with just the outline of the mountains and the moon shining above them outside the windows. Tori led me through a doorway into her bedroom with a bed against the wall topped with big, fluffy pillows and a quilt.

She stopped at the foot of the bed before turning to face me. Once again, she looked a little uncertain. I wanted to know all the answers, to understand her.

"This is my bedroom," she announced. She shook her head and rolled her eyes, a little giggle slipping out, the sound itself spinning around my heart.

"Is it now?" I teased lightly.

She giggled again, and I loved the pink flush on her cheeks. "I always leave a lamp on." She gestured to the lamp that was, in fact, turned on over beside the bed on the nightstand.

"So let's have this conversation first," she announced.

"What conversation?"

"Birth control," she said flatly.

"I have a condom," I said, because I always did.

Not that I got all that much action, especially not since I'd been helping take care of my mom, but old habits die hard and all that. My mom had been a stickler about that and had sat me down to give me a whole lecture about birth control and STDs and safety and protection and health and so on. Since I'd been a teenager at the time, awkward didn't even come close to capturing how I'd felt, but I'd taken every word she said to heart.

Tori took a quick breath as she nodded. "Okay. It's um.." She twisted her hands together in front of her before clearing her throat. "Not a big thing, I guess, but I do get checked every year just to be safe. And, it's been, well, a while," she added.

"We have to get checked at our annual physical. It's protocol. I guess it makes it easier," I said with a shrug.

"Okay." Her shoulders rose with a breath.

"It's been a while for me too," I added, because it only seemed fair since she was being vulnerable.

Her brows rose, her gaze sharp and skeptical. "I don't believe you."

I shrugged. "Believe it. Tori, I'm a hotshot firefighter. I just moved here a little while ago, and I live with my mom because I help take care of her, because she has health issues."

"I'm sorry to hear that," Tori cut in.

"No need to be sorry. She's okay. She just needs a little help, and I'm happy to do it. That wasn't really something I had to think about. All this to say, I don't have much time."

She angled her head to the side. "You're a good man, Kincaid. Do you need to let your mom know where you are?"

"Now?" A startled laugh sputtered out of me. "No, I don't. She knows I'm at the fundraiser and that's enough. She'll watch her favorite shows on her TV in her bedroom in the in-law apartment that she stays in. It's built off the side of the main house because that's what she wanted, and she won't worry about where I am because that's not her style."

"Oh, oh," Tori said. I could practically see her brain trying to sort all of these details into her mental idea of me.

"Are we done with this conversation?" I asked after silence fell again and began to stretch.

She nodded quickly. "Yes, we are."

"Now, where were we?" I murmured.

# Chapter Fourteen

# TORI

*Now, where were we?*

Kincaid's voice alone was enough to send a hot shiver down my spine. But with him standing here in my bedroom, every inch of his muscular body close was the equivalent of human catnip.

He took a step closer, and I reflexively stepped back, mostly because the force of his presence was so intense. My hips bumped into the bed. He leaned forward, resting his hands on either side of me, caging me between his arms.

"Now, I want you to forget everything except how good you feel," he murmured, his voice rumbly and gruff, sizzling over my nerves. "Don't hesitate to tell me what you want, to tell me what you like."

My belly did a little swoop, and I all but melted right there. Sex had been "meh" for the most part for me. Okay was the best I could offer for my past experiences, nothing great, nothing to write home about.

Usually, the beginning felt better and then, well, it was like the womp-womp-womp sound in a movie when something failed to live up to expectations, or when a scene ended in benign disappointment. I didn't even know how to say what I wanted because, well, that wasn't something that had ever worked out.

All I could manage to do was nod. Kincaid straightened again, lifting a hand and hooking his finger over at the V at the top of my blouse. I could feel the brush of his knuckle against my skin, the subtle touch like the lick of a flame.

"Let's get this out of the way," he murmured.

In that moment, I decided, because I wasn't sure what else to do, to just abandon myself to this process. I felt safe with Kincaid. Although that detail was slightly terrifying for a corner of my mind and heart, I clung to it. I didn't want to overthink. I didn't want to let my brain get in the way.

Kincaid began to unwrap me like a present. He moved in increments, one button at a time on my blouse, his lips brushing over my skin, nipping at an earlobe, teasing on the side of my neck. He dropped hot kisses after each button came undone and revealed another small patch of skin until the last kiss landed just above the waistband of my skirt.

In this moment, my clothing felt constricting. I wanted to throw everything off, get everything out of the way. Each kiss was like a drop of scalding hot honey on my skin, the heat radiating outward in slow motion. He straightened, his dark eyes burning into mine as I stood there in my bra and skirt.

He startled me when he dipped his head, and his mouth closed over a nipple through the silky lace of my bra. The hot shock of it drew a cry from my mouth. He lifted his head, a wicked gleam in his eyes, just as he reached between my breasts. With a deft twist, he released the clasp on my bra.

My breath was short, my brain lightheaded from the lack of oxygen, and I cried out again when he teased my other nipple. The next few moments passed in a hazy blur.

He started slow, but by the time he peeled my skirt off and I stumbled as I kicked them free from my ankles, the look in his eyes was as wild and untethered as mine. I yanked at his shirt, and he reached behind his head to lift it up and over swiftly without even unbuttoning it.

I let out a sigh of relief when he stepped close, and I could finally feel his bare skin hot under my touch, his hardness against my softness. I let my hands explore the muscled planes of his chest, smoothing over his abs before clasping around his back to feel his corded strength there.

He stepped back, and I almost cried out in protest, but he said, "Just a sec," as he pulled his wallet out of his back pocket, moving quickly before tossing a condom on the bed.

A moment later, I impatiently undid the buttons of his fly. He gave me an assist, stumbling as I shoved his jeans down around his hips. His chuckle was low, and almost wondering, when his eyes lifted to mine.

"Tori," he murmured, "you're literally going to bring me to my knees."

I couldn't help the giggle that slipped out. His eyes narrowed as he stepped closer, his hands curling on my hips as he lifted me up on the bed, stepping between my knees.

I was down to nothing but a pair of practical cotton panties, while he was down to a pair of fitted boxer briefs. Every inch of Kincaid was muscle, and I took the moment to study him. He was tall with a lean frame. I knew his job demanded fitness, but even then, there was an edge to him, almost a leashed strength and energy, even when he was still.

My fingers trailed over a jagged scar on one of his shoulders. "A branch," he offered. "Not even when I was working. I was hiking and slipped on a rock."

"Oh," I whispered.

My exploring fingers discovered another scar, this one along the edge of his ribs.

When my eyes lifted to his in question, he explained, "I was working for that one. Rocks are unforgiving."

I leaned close and pressed a kiss on it, savoring the sound of air drawing in through his teeth. I dragged my palm over his thick length, eliciting another hiss of his breath. He dipped his head, nipping lightly on the side of my neck. I shivered, arching into his touch like a purring cat.

Once again, it felt as if a flame spun around me, catching me in its heat, like fire with oxygen pouring in. His touch kindled the heat higher and hotter. His lips blazed a trail down my neck, teasing my nipples, mapping over my trembling belly.

Somewhere along the way, he shifted me back, his hand flattening as he slid it down between my breasts, a teasing touch of his thumb on one. The calloused surface of his palm sent sparks leaping over my skin. He murmured something against my belly before his fingers hooked on the edge of my panties.

I distantly heard him tell me, "Lift your hips."

Without hesitation, I did as he asked, because I would have done *anything* he asked in this moment. He dragged them down over my legs, and I heard the sound of the fabric rumpling to the floor. On the heels of a gasping breath, his palms were sliding up my calves before I felt them pressing my thighs apart.

I was breathless and needy, so, so needy. He dropped hot kisses on the insides of my calves and then thighs. Who knew that skin just where my knee bent was so wildly sensitive? Not me. Ever. I was shivering and trembling, each kiss like a hot pebble dropped in a pond, the sensation and heat radiating outward.

"Tori..."

At the sound of his gruff voice, I dragged my eyes open, meeting his.

His fingers teased into the slick wetness of my sex, and I bit my lip, unable to keep a whimper from escaping. He sank two fingers inside of me. I cried out again when he drew them out and licked my arousal off of them. It was a good thing I was already lying down on a bed, because I would have completely combusted and melted on the spot. Seconds later, he brought his mouth to my sex, and proceeded to drive me simply out of my mind.

Lazy licks with his tongue, teasing pumps with his fingers, exploring me slowly and languidly, pushing me to the edge. I lost all sense of time. All I knew was that I was chasing the relief from the pressure building inside. A sense of pleasure drew tighter and tighter. I could feel it building, the tease of it so intense, until I begged, "Kincaid, please..."

My voice was a rasp, broken by my gasps. One deep pump of his fingers, and I felt the graze of his teeth over my clit. He sucked lightly, and everything that was drawing tight inside broke apart with a piercing burst of pleasure. I was shuddering all over, my fingers flexing against the comforter as I cried out.

I was near liquid and boneless by the time the intensity of the pleasure abated. I was gasping, still trying to catch my breath. I distantly absorbed the sense of him moving, my eyes dragging open to see him rolling on the condom he'd had the foresight to toss on the bed.

His weight eased over me, and I savored the feel of it when he brought his mouth to mine with a lazy kiss. I could taste myself on him, the subtle salty tang. I loved it.

"Tori," he rasped, and I dragged my eyes open. "Is this still okay?"

I could feel his thick crown pressing at my entrance. As if it could be anything other than okay. But I understood he was asking, and he wanted an answer.

My head barely moved as I whispered, "Yes, please..."

I was begging. Again. Because even though he had just given me the most intense orgasm I'd ever had, I wanted more. "I want all of it. Please," I added as he held my gaze.

I cried out at the sensation of him filling me in a slow thrust.

# Chapter Fifteen

# KINCAID

*I want all of it. Please.*

Tori's eyes were dark, and I nearly came at the feel of her clenching around me as I seated myself deeply inside of her.

I held still for a beat. She took a shaky breath along with me. I had to keep still for several moments, just to keep from coming inside of her instantly. She felt so good with her knees rising up, one foot curling around my calf.

She was still trembling from her orgasm. I felt the press of her fingers along my back, and after a few more beats, she rocked her hips impatiently. I usually had more control, but control had spun out of my reach long moments ago when I tasted her. Now, inside of her, I felt caught in the rush of a current I couldn't slow down. All I could do was ride it and try to keep my head above water.

I drew back, sinking in again, and she cried out, arching her hips into mine. When I heard her whisper my name, it was like lightning cracking across the sky of the storm surrounding us, sizzling through me. I felt the light nip of her teeth on the side of my neck. She said my name again, followed by "please," and the current crashed over me. My release was gathering force, tightening at the base of my spine before snapping loose when another bolt of lightning sizzled across the sky.

She cried out when I barely remembered to reach between us, because I needed her to fall into this release with me. I could feel her crest when I pressed over her clit, teasing with my fingers.

It was messy, and I had zero finesse, but it was enough. She clamped down around me, and that was it. We were trembling together for long moments.

I didn't even know how much time passed in the haze of that fiery release when I collapsed against her, barely remembering to roll over so I didn't crush her. It felt as if we'd crash-landed together after the rush of a storm. The air was clearing, and we held still together to catch our breath.

———

I was dozing with Tori soft against my side, both of us resting, feeling almost cast adrift on a soothing current. I was entirely sated to a degree I'd never experienced before. Gradually, I managed to shake myself out of my haze and get up to walk into the bathroom adjacent to her bedroom.

The bathroom was small, but tidy, with a tub and shower opposite the sink. I quickly disposed of my condom and washed my hands.

Tori followed me into the room a moment later, and when I turned to face her, my heart gave a spinning kick in my chest. There was so much to this that I didn't know how to absorb. She studied me for a beat, her skin still flushed and her eyes dark.

"I need to walk Bella," she said after the moment began to stretch between us.

"Okay," I replied.

Moments later, we both tugged on our clothing and went out into the yard. Bella padded alongside Tori at a leisurely pace. She did her business and then turned toward us, clearly expecting affection. Tori didn't hesitate, lavishing her with kisses and strokes on her face.

When we walked back inside, Bella promptly curled up on her bed in the living room. Tori checked the wood stove, making sure the fire was low, before straightening and asking, "Do you want to stay?"

# Chapter Sixteen

# TORI

*Do you want to stay?*

My own question to Kincaid reverberated in my thoughts the following morning as I came awake slowly. I felt deeply rested and relaxed. I couldn't recall why for a moment. My mind was blank for a few beats before I began to catalogue the feel of Kincaid beside me.

I was pressed against him, my head tucked into the curve of his shoulder. His arm was loosely curled around me, and I felt his palm resting on the side of my hip. I felt deliciously good. I loved the feel of him strong against my side.

Not wanting to break the moment, I took in a careful breath. I could see out the windows from where I was resting against him. The mountains were silhouetted by the shimmering sun just along the edges. Sunrise would be here soon. I loved spring in Alaska. It was beautiful. It felt like the world was bursting with life after the quiet, dark months of winter.

Although I didn't want to disrupt this moment, my bladder had other opinions. I eased away from Kincaid, carefully rolling out of bed and tiptoeing into the bathroom. After I took care of business, I washed my hands and splashed water on my face.

I'd been cursed with being one of those people who really never fell back asleep once I woke. Much as I wanted to return to bed and feel sleepy again, I knew I was likely awake for the day now.

I studied myself in the mirror for a moment. My cheeks were still pink with the flush of sleep, and my hair was a mess of tangled locks.

Just as I was contemplating hopping in the shower, I heard Kincaid's voice. "Tori?"

I opened the door, and it felt like my body came awake instantly, every cell coming alive like the rise of a flock of birds shifting suddenly from the ground into motion with a cacophony of calls. Kincaid's hair was mussed, and he had a shadow of stubble on his jaw. He stood there in his boxers, his muscled arms relaxed at his sides.

"Hi," I said, instantly flushing.

Because what a silly thing to say, as though I was greeting him. As though what had passed between us last night had never happened.

"Good morning," he returned with a smile teasing the corners of his mouth.

With my body humming, I held his gaze as heat suffused me. My belly felt all tingly, and my heart felt flipped over in my chest. When my eyes dipped down, they landed on the lengthening swell of his arousal.

Without thinking—something that I was discovering happened with Kincaid often—I reached for his hand. "Let's shower," I murmured.

Moments later, the hot water was cascading around us, and Kincaid's hands were smoothing over my sides. I spun around, giggling a little. "Good morning," I belatedly offered.

His low chuckle spun into the sensations ricocheting through me. "It *is* a good morning," he replied.

I traced my fingertip along the stubbled edge of his jaw before dipping my head to press kisses along his collarbone. I was gratified at the sound of his breath sucking in through his teeth.

"Tori," he murmured, his voice gruff and sending goosebumps over my skin.

Everything with Kincaid was a different sensation, drawing a different reaction from my body. All of them were oriented towards two things—him and this feeling between us.

I lightly trailed my fingertips over his chest and abs before curling my palm around his length and stroking. His breath hissed through his teeth again, and I pressed him back. I heard his hand slap against the wall.

I didn't hesitate and leaned down, lightly teasing my tongue around the tip of his shaft. His fingers laced in my wet hair.

"Tori," he growled.

My only answer was, "Mmm-hmm?" around his cock as I sucked him into my mouth.

His fingers tightened in my hair. I knelt down, angling my head to the side to glance up as I drew away and released him with a little pop.

"You don't have to—" he began.

I cut him off. "I want to." On the heels of a breath, I sucked him in again. I felt his shaft pulse as I dragged my tongue along the underside. Adding a little suction when I reached the tip again, I curled my palm loosely around his length. I stroked up and down as I teased him. He muttered something unintelligible, and I hummed a little bit in reply.

I felt his cock pulse again, and the taste of his release danced over my tongue. Just before I sucked him in once more, and he jerked. His fingers gripped even more tightly in my hair. I drew back as his release spurted out over my hand and down onto my chest.

When I looked up at him, his eyes were dark and his breath coming in heaves. He slowly eased his grip in my hair and pulled me up to standing. We tumbled into a kiss.

Kincaid spun us around, pressing me against the wall as he

deftly teased his fingers into my folds. I was already wet. I had been since I'd woken. Now, with his fingers pumping in and out of my channel, I was gasping, clinging to him as he fucked me with his fingers. Somehow, he knew just when to give me the right amount of pressure with his thumb exactly where I needed it. I cried out, shuddering and barely able to stand as I sagged against the tiled wall.

I stared at him, my breath coming in ragged gasps. "That was fast," I finally managed.

Kincaid's smile was a little wicked. "Well, I could say the same."

Before I knew it, I was giggling with a sense of giddiness rising like champagne bubbles inside.

We properly showered after that, before getting dressed and going downstairs. It was still early, but now the sun's rays were breaking in an arc over the mountains.

Bella was still sound asleep. "Does she ever move from that bed?" Kincaid asked, eyeing her affectionately.

"Sometimes. She used to sleep in my bed with me, but she can't jump up anymore." I felt a little sad whenever I thought about that sign of her age. "I know she can't live forever, but she's my best friend. I'm hoping for some kind of miracle."

His eyes were warm as he held my gaze. "She seems pretty healthy for her age. How old did you say she was?"

"Almost fourteen. The vet says she's in good shape with no major health problems other than arthritis."

"Well, there you go," he said with a soft smile.

We fell quiet. The silence stretched between us—not uncomfortable, exactly, but uncertain, at least for me. It was a kind of uncertainty that stemmed from something bigger.

I had never actually spent a full night with a man before. I wasn't some sheltered innocent when it came to sex. And yet, no one had ever meant enough for me to feel comfortable having them stay.

"I need to get home, just to check on my mom," he finally said.

"And report back on your whereabouts for the night?" I teased lightly.

His lips curled at the corners as he shrugged slightly. "Not quite. She doesn't expect me to report in. But I do like to check in and make sure she's doing okay every morning."

He took a breath, his shoulders rising with it. I could tell he was working through something in his mind and waited. "I want to see you again, Tori," he said softly.

"Oh, I'm sure you will." My voice sounded chirpy, as if I'd been surprised mid-sneeze. I tried to rally and sound casual. I was desperate, for myself, not to seem as if this was as big of a deal as it felt inside. "I mean, it's a small town. It'll be hard not to see you."

Kincaid smiled faintly. "But I meant *see* you. Like, take you out to dinner, lunch, breakfast—whatever you want."

I blinked. I didn't know why this surprised me, but it did. "Okay," I said, clearing my throat. "I feel like I should point this out right now, just so we're crystal clear—I don't do the whole 'seeing multiple people at a time' thing."

"I haven't dated anybody in, well, not since I started taking care of my mom." He shook his head slightly.

"I just wanted to put that out there," I added, so uncertain how to handle my own feelings here. I liked Kincaid. Probably way more than I should.

"To clarify, it's been years since I dated. I've never tried to 'see' multiple people at a time," he replied.

As soon as he added that, I noticed the discomfort in his expression. He shifted slightly, like maybe he'd said too much.

Even if our reasons were entirely different, it helped to sense his discomfort. It wasn't that I wanted him to feel uncomfortable, but more that I didn't feel so alone in how vulnerable I felt. He didn't need to know just how hung up I was on trust, or how the very idea of relying on anyone else emotionally in any way was terrifying for me.

"I know this is fresh. I don't have expectations. I'm not saying—" I started and then stopped abruptly.

He stepped closer and reached for my hand. His touch was instantly grounding. His thumb brushed a slow motion over my knuckles. "I know it's just been one night. One date, and two kisses before that, but I like you. I'm not saying we need to make it more serious than it is. I just, well, I felt like I should be clear." He let out a breath. "I've never done the online dating thing, but I hear it's a nightmare with people playing games and mixed expectations. So I just wanted you to know, I'm not that kind of guy."

"I know you're not that guy."

"You do?"

I bit my lip and nodded. "I guess I do know that about you. You're a good man, Kincaid."

————

While my doubts clamored in the corners of my mind over the following days, I kept trying to remind myself of one thing: I *did* believe Kincaid was a good man. My gut trusted him.

And yet, I remembered—before I found out about my dad and Shelly—I would have bet my soul that neither of them could ever betray the people who loved them. But they had. For an entire decade.

And, doubt? Doubt was a mean girl and practically a professional in my thoughts. My doubts were old and well-formed. They knew the routine and how to make sure I questioned everything and everyone.

# Chapter Seventeen

# KINCAID

"You spent the night," my mother pointed out.

She waited four whole days since I stayed with Tori to remind me of this. "I know, Mom. I'm an adult. Do I need to remind you of that again? It's not like I'm even a fresh adult, I'm thirty-three years old."

"I know, I know," my mother exclaimed. "I'm just, you know, I'm excited. You haven't had a "relationship"."

She used air quotes around the word relationship. I sat down at the small round table in the kitchen and sighed.

"Mom, I haven't...ugh." I ran a hand through my hair. "I dated some in high school, and college, and here and there, but the life of a hotshot firefighter isn't great for long-term relationships. I've had other priorities."

"So you're saying you don't have a relationship with Tori?"

I rolled my eyes and flattened my palm on the table with a muted thump. "Mom. We went on one date. To a fundraiser. And yes, I spent the night."

She opened her mouth, but I cut her off. "I like Tori. A lot. But I don't know what's going to happen. For God's sake, please don't go around town acting like we're about to get married. You're going to chase her off if you do."

My mother's brows hitched high as she studied me. Her mouth dropped open slightly before she let out a satisfied little huff. "Oh. So it matters if I chase her off?"

"Oh, my God, Mom," I warned. I leaned my head back, staring at the ceiling like it might offer me divine assistance with this moment. Bringing my gaze back to my mother, I replied, "I like Tori. I would like the opportunity to see where things go."

"Willow Brook is full of firefighters. Seems like a great place for you to have a relationship," she pointed out in her helpful tone.

"What?" I sputtered.

"Yes!" she said, nodding emphatically. "I've met plenty of them—Beck, Levi, Graham—he has kids! He was a single dad before he met Madison. Cooper, Griffin, so many of them. They're all good guys, and they're all in committed relationships."

"I know, Mom," I replied, trying to keep my frustration out of my voice. "Could you just relax about this?"

"I just want you to be happy."

"I am happy," I ground out. Because I was. I *was* content with the life I had.

Maybe. But maybe Tori made me want things I hadn't even contemplated before. That said, I didn't need my mother sharing her theories about my potential love life with everyone from the gas station to the grocery store.

"Can you just let things play out for me? Please."

"Yes." My mother straightened in her chair and clasped her hands together. I knew that meant she was feeling gleeful. God help me.

"So anyway," I said, trying to get back on track. "The whole point of this was me letting you know I'm going out to dinner tonight, and I may or may not come home after that."

"Oh, my gosh!" Now, she clapped her hands, looking downright delighted. "I hope you don't come home. I hope it's amazing. I want you to fall in love!"

I took a slow breath, gritting my teeth. "I love you, Mom. But please—I'm begging you—please don't make things complicated."

She let out a heavy sigh just as the doorbell rang. "That'll be Chris," she said, calling toward the door. She shouted for him to come in. As soon as he stepped into the kitchen, she beamed up at him, and I braced myself.

"Chris, Kincaid has a second date. He already spent the night with her!"

"Yeah, you told me that, Claudia," Chris replied, barely concealing his laugh.

"Oh, my God, Mom." With a groan, I dropped my face into my hands and ran them through my hair, letting them fall to the table with a thump. "Chris, could you please get her to stop gossiping about my love life?"

Chris grinned as he leaned down to kiss my mom on the cheek. Straightening again, he eyed me. "It's a small town, man. I'm sure your mom isn't the only one who knows you two went out. You were at the fundraiser. That was a big event for Willow Brook." He held up a hand, as if preemptively preparing me. "Someone else saw your truck leaving her driveway the next morning."

"Oh my God..." That was all I could say to that.

"Buttons?" I prompted.

The little hamster sitting on the floor blinked up at me expectantly. Lucy stopped beside me, and as always, I felt gigantic standing next to her. She was petite with her delicate build, but her personality was anything but tiny. She ran one of the best construction companies in town with her best friend, Amelia, and she didn't take any nonsense from anyone.

Levi, who had been a few years ahead of me in high school—and, at the time, known for being probably the biggest flirt in school—walked through the kitchen and stopped beside Lucy. He pressed a lingering kiss to her cheek. "I'll be back."

Lucy smiled up at him. "Of course you'll be back."

Amelia chuckled as she reached for a drink. "Now that's some faith."

"She knows I'm still whipped," Levi said dryly. "Mom says Glory is set for the night with her," he added before heading down the hallway.

"My mom has our daughter for the night," Lucy added. "She loves it. In fact, she says being a grandmother is more fun than being a parent."

"It seems like most people agree with that," Jasmine chimed in as she approached.

When I felt a nudge on my ankle, I glanced down to see the hamster curiously sniffing me. "So, why the name Buttons?" I asked.

"Because he likes to eat buttons. Or, well, play with them," Lucy explained with a laugh.

"What does he do with them?" Luna asked, intrigued.

Levi's chuckle echoed back from the hallway. "He collects them."

A moment later, Levi was gone. As we filtered toward the kitchen table, Lucy elaborated, "After Ham passed..." She pressed a hand to her heart. "Who we loved. Levi was so sad. Ham was his special hamster."

"So it took a while before he was ready for another one," Amelia added.

Lucy nodded emphatically. "One day we were at a store, and a woman was giving away a hamster. Just one—Buttons."

As if summoned by the mention of his name, Buttons came scampering over. Lucy tossed a couple of pieces of lettuce into a bowl in the corner, and the hamster made a beeline for it.

"Anyway, we got him home, and we kept finding things with missing buttons, off shirts, coats. Took us forever to realize he was the thief. He'd been collecting them."

She gestured toward his cage—though "cage" wasn't really accurate. It looked like a hamster luxury condo, multi-leveled and full of toys. "And, there they all are." In the corner of his little hamster condo was a stash of buttons.

A laugh sputtered out of me as I sat down beside Casey. "Buttons is so cute. I've never known anyone to have a hamster just running loose."

"Levi insists on it," Lucy said with a sigh. "I'm constantly worried I'm going to step on him. But Ham was happy that way, and Buttons seems to be doing just great." She cast a bemused smile toward Buttons.

We settled around the table, occasionally noshing off the tray of nachos Lucy had set out. "These are amazing," I commented between bites.

Amelia snorted and rolled her eyes. "Lucy definitely did not make these."

Lucy shrugged nonchalantly. "I don't cook. But Levi does."

As the evening wore on, the crowd expanded. By the time we had settled into a card game, there were nine women there, most of whom I'd grown up with, except for a few newcomers. Lucy, Amelia, Maisie, Holly, Tish, Casey, Luna, and Jasmine.

Maisie turned out to be the most serious of the card players. She won hand after hand, and she didn't even blink while she was at it.

I smiled over at Casey, who was seated beside me. "Thanks for encouraging me to finally come."

She grinned and wrapped an arm around my shoulders, giving me a quick squeeze before leaning back in her chair. "You were due. I even come to these. Elsa moved back, and she's been coming when she can. So it's important."

"What's going on with you and Kincaid?" Maisie's question came out of nowhere.

When I glanced over, her eyes were still locked on her cards. Her question threw me off. I hadn't expected anyone to bring Kincaid up.

"What do you mean?" I hedged.

"Well, you were his date for the fundraiser," she said casually, playing her next card before finally lifting her gaze to mine. "I like Kincaid. He takes care of his mom."

"I know," I said, nodding.

"Beck keeps me up to speed," Maisie added.

"He's going to ask you about him soon enough," Casey said. "He was already giving Kincaid relationship advice at the station."

"Beck?" I blinked.

"Beck is the office gossip," Amelia chimed in, her tone dry. "Or at least, that's what the guys call him."

I laughed, genuinely startled. "Are you serious?"

"Completely," Tish piped up from the far side of the table. "He means well, though. The man went from competing with Levi for the biggest flirt in high school to being a dedicated family man."

Maisie's gaze sobered when she glanced up. "He really is. Now, he's convinced everyone will just be happier if they settle down. He says kids aren't required—because there are plenty to babysit."

Lucy rolled her eyes. "Beck can babysit for me whenever he wants."

"We don't need to babysit anyone," Maisie said hurriedly. "Two is enough."

"Anyway," Amelia cut in, leaning forward, "back to Tori. How are you and Kincaid? I mean, it could have just been a date..."

My mind immediately flashed back to that night after the fundraiser.

"Oh, it was more than a date," Casey teased.

"How do you... Why are you saying that?" I sputtered.

"Because you're blushing," she sing-songed. "You wouldn't be blushing if it was just a one-off date."

"So?" Maisie prompted, tilting her head.

My shoulders lifted with a subtle shrug. "You all know my story. Or, I guess, my parents' story."

"Oh, yeah," Holly said with a little snort. "And, Shelly's moved back to town. She's going around telling anyone who'll listen how sad she is that she lost her best friend."

"Oh, for fuck's sake, Shelly," someone muttered.

I appreciated the sentiment.

"So, what happened?" Tish asked, her voice careful. "I don't know the story because I only moved here recently. Although if you don't want to talk about it, I understand."

I desperately did not want to delve into it, but it was what it was. Thankfully, Amelia jumped in quickly. "Tori's dad had an affair with her mom's best friend. For, like, a decade. Nobody knew—until *everybody* knew. Then, he left and married the best friend. After that, he had an affair on her. Sometimes karma bites back fast."

Tish's eyes went wide. "Oh." Her brow furrowed when she looked toward me again. "I'm so sorry."

I twisted my lips to the side, shrugging lightly. "No need to apologize. It sucked for my mom and me, but life goes on."

Maisie pursed her lips and shook her head. "I hadn't heard that until Cade and Beck told me what happened. So hurtful."

"He worked with Cade's dad," Amelia explained. "Rex is still pissed." Amelia's gaze swung to me, the concern clear in her eyes. "We don't have to talk about it," she added gently. "But I find things lose their power when we just put them out there. Takes all the oomph away."

"Honestly? Thank you. It's easier if I don't have to explain." It really did feel like a bracing breath of fresh air. The gust of the truth blew away some of the shame I still carried, even though none of it had been mine to bear. I had just been caught in the swirl of everything I believed about my family going down the drain.

"How's your mom handling Shelly being here?" Amelia asked.

"Better than me," I admitted, sighing. "She says they'll never be friends again, but she's let it go. Because she wants peace. Shelly, on the other hand, keeps trying to talk to me."

"Maybe just talk to her so you can sweep it away, like dust under a sofa or something," Amelia offered.

Holly's nose wrinkled. "That's one way to describe it. But—" She eyed me, her gaze considering. "I imagine trust isn't easy."

"Oh, my God, no," I said flatly. "I'm not really looking for a relationship," I added after a pause. "I'm not sure I ever will be."

"I get that," Maisie said. "Maybe someday it'll feel right. And, if it does feel right, I think Kincaid's a great guy."

Blessedly, that seemed to be that—for now, at least—for

curiosity about me and Kincaid. Conversation rumbled on, covering everything from Amelia and Lucy's building projects to how long it took Elsa to find a new washer and dryer set.

Eventually, Casey leaned in again. "You won't believe this. Remember how I mentioned the woman with the divorce party?"

"Oh yeah, I waited on them," I replied.

"Anyway, she's moving here."

"Seriously?"

"Yep."

"Good for her," I said.

"So if you see her around town, be nice and welcoming," Casey said. "She's not officially here yet, but she was flying back to 'the scene of the crime,' as she put it, and she's planning to come back for another trip."

I left that evening feeling filled up in a way I hadn't in a long time. Not just from the nachos and the laughter, but from something deeper. Even my emotions around friendship had been tangled and bitter for years. Because Shelly—well, she hadn't just been a friend of my mom's, she had been *that* friend. The one my mom turned to for everything. Her confidante. Her sister in everything but blood. Her actions had ruined it so painfully. Even though she hadn't been my best friend, I knew how much she'd meant to my mom, and I'd watched what the betrayal did.

That night, as I lay in bed, I kept thinking about the group around the table. I couldn't imagine any of them doing what Shelly had done. Maybe that was naive. Maybe not.

I knew I needed to have the conversation with Shelly eventually, to air it out, to get it over with. But I just wasn't quite there yet. My emotional capacity was already pretty maxed out.

A few days after that card night, despite all my best efforts to play it cool, to keep it totally casual, I spent another night with Kincaid.

One night turned into two, and then three. Not every night, maybe every third night, one of us would text.

*You up?*

*Can I see you tonight?*

The other would always say yes. I knew better. My mind knew better. But my heart was definitely not listening. It had been a stretch of four full weeks now. Four weeks that felt like a lifetime.

I was due to get my period. I was very regular. Usually.

My mom studied me from across the kitchen table. I had stopped by her apartment to check in after coming home from a night with Tori.

"And, how is Tori?" my mother asked brightly, before taking a swallow of her coffee.

"She's great, Mom. How are you? That's why I stopped by."

"I'm great."

I bit back a laugh as I sat down across from her. After a moment, her gaze sobered, and she tilted her head to the side, studying me.

"What's that look for?" I asked.

"I spoke to your father."

My chest tightened. "What?" I asked, my tone sharp.

"Yep, I did. He's no longer here in Alaska."

"I told you I expected that," I pointed out.

"But he'd like to talk to you," she added.

"Why now?" I knew all along—because my mother wasn't one to dance around secrets—that she had hoped he was still around, that we'd reconnect somehow. Or, connect at all.

It wasn't that I was opposed to the idea, but I had honestly, I suppose, assumed it would never happen. He'd known about my existence. He just never cared.

"Where is he?" I asked, striving to keep my tone level.

"Apparently, he's in Seattle near his family. He also has medical issues, but they're more serious than mine."

"Is that supposed to make me feel bad?" I knew my voice sounded defensive, but I didn't even try to hide it.

My mom set her coffee mug on the table and reached across, catching one of my hands in both of hers before squeezing and releasing it.

"No, it's not supposed to make you feel guilty. I just want you to know what's happening. I'm not trying to pressure you. But when you were younger, you always wanted to at least talk to him."

I stayed quiet, mostly because I didn't know what to say.

"I'm not saying that's what you should do, but the door is finally open," she said gently. "Think about it. I can be on the call with you."

I knew that would help, and yet, I also felt reluctant. "I'll think about it," I finally said.

My mom opened her mouth to speak again, but I narrowed my eyes and shook my head slightly. "Let me think about it, Mom. In the meantime, as I've told you since I was old enough to have an opinion—feel free to tell him whatever you want about me if he asks. I don't have anything to hide."

Her eyes were a little damp, and I ignored the twist in my chest. This was one of those messy, tangled, emotional topics for both of us. I knew she'd been trying to connect with him for years. She'd done it because I'd told her I had wanted to talk to him when I was little, long ago. And now, she'd found him.

I suspected part of her thought this was the healthy next step for me. That a conversation might help me heal some invisible wound. But I needed space. I didn't want to hurt her either. The complicated situation looped back into itself.

I reached over for her hand, squeezing this time with reassurance. "I promise, Mom. I will think about it, and I'll probably talk to him."

I saw the hopefulness in her gaze and quickly added, "I just need a minute. More than a minute."

"I love you, Kincaid," she said somberly.

"And, I love you, Mom. You're the best parent anyone could've asked for."

———

I didn't usually see Tori two nights in a row. We had fallen into a pattern—every other night, maybe every third. No expectations. No pressure. But tonight, I felt an emotional pull to see her.

I needed to lose myself in her. In this unexpected connection that had taken hold and kept strengthening. In the bonds that were tightening between us, even though I had no idea what to do about them.

I knew she was working, so she wouldn't check her phone until the end of her shift. I headed out to the winery and snagged a table in her section. She was efficient and on-task, like always, when she was working. But her eyes had a warm glint, and her lips teased with a flirty smile when she stopped beside my table, handing me the specials menu and filling my water.

"Well, Mr. Green, what can I get you tonight?" she asked. Her voice was low and throaty, and it slid over my unsettled nerves, soothing me.

"I was actually hoping I could just wait for you until you got off shift tonight."

Her eyes widened slightly before her brow furrowed. "Are you okay?"

"Is it so wrong that I want to see you tonight?" I countered, ignoring the pinch in my heart. I didn't even know how to comprehend the way she immediately sensed something was off with me.

"Of course not. I always love to see you, Kincaid," she said lightly, tapping her notepad with her pencil. "Do you know what you want?"

"I'll take the salmon burger. What time do you get off tonight?"

Her eyes flicked to the large clock mounted above the bar. "I'm on the early shift. Just another hour."

"Perfect."

———

*One hour later*

The glow from Tori's taillights was a little beacon in the falling darkness. As I followed her back to her house, my pulse ticked along like a metronome—steady and fast—because I knew what lay ahead.

I needed this. I needed *her*. I needed to lose myself in the fire of our connection, in the intimacy that felt as if it were binding us tighter together. When I turned onto the driveway, the rumble of gravel under my tires spun into the hum inside my body. I parked beside her car, warmth slipping through me as I climbed out.

I knew the routine now. She would let Bella out, and her sweet dog would meander for a few minutes, sniffing the grass and trees before she did her business. When we walked inside, Tori always took a few moments to lavish Bella with pets and murmured affection. Only then would Bella come over to greet me, sitting down slowly in front of me with that patient, expectant look in her warm brown eyes. After that, she'd walk over to her bed, curl up, and fall asleep with complete trust in her world.

Once Bella was settled, Tori hung up her jacket. I followed suit, and we both left our shoes by the door. She tipped her head slightly, her gaze studying me, and it felt like she could read straight into my unsettled thoughts.

"Are you okay?" Her voice was soft, a little raspy.

One shoulder lifted in a shrug as I took a breath, steadying myself inside. "Yeah," I finally said.

She opened her mouth to say something else, but I added more before she could. I surprised myself. "My mom talked to my dad."

Tori's eyes widened slightly, her brows rising. "Oh. Do you want to talk about it?"

She reached for me, her palm curling around mine. Her thumb slid in a slow, soothing stroke over the back of my hand.

I shook my head.

"Okay," she said simply.

The tension wound tightly inside eased a little. I needed her understanding.

Beyond that, I just needed this connection. I needed her. She dropped my hand, placing her palm right in the center of my chest. I felt my heart lurch forward, as if her touch itself was tugging it closer.

She dipped her head and pressed her lips into the hollow at the base of my throat—just like she had the night we first kissed. The heat of her kiss radiated outward, like slow ripples from a small pebble dropped into water. I was wordless, caught in a maelstrom of need and emotion.

Without saying a word, she stepped back and reached for my hand. I followed her up the stairs, onto the landing, and into her bedroom. She stopped, turning to face me.

"I probably smell like food," she said with a low, sheepish laugh.

I chuckled. "Well, the food there is really good," I offered.

The sound of her throaty laugh was like champagne fizzing inside of me. "It is good," she agreed.

All rational thought dissolved in the heat of our connection when she stepped closer again. In a matter of seconds, we were plastered together. I needed to feel her, needed to be grounded in our connection. As the moments unfolded, second by second, each a tick of the metronome, the need between us burned hot and fast. There was almost a wildness to it whenever we were close.

In spite of the wild edge, or perhaps because of it, it was also grounding for me. Because I could forget everything else but sensation. Her silky hands mapping my body. The feel of her lips underneath mine. Claiming her mouth with kiss after kiss. The sound of her breath rasping with mine. The feel of her soft curves. The contrast to my hardness. The press of her nipples. The flush of her skin. The way desire unfurled between us. The push and pull of our connection. When I teased my fingers into her slippery folds. The sound of her soft sigh. The way her breath hitched in her throat. The way she nipped the side of my neck. Her touch was sure as her palms slid over my chest and abs to curl around my length. The way her eyes met mine in the dim light.

When she rose up over me and said, "This right here," I was so lost in the moment that I forgot to put a condom on.

Just as she slid over the underside of my cock, and I almost came instantly, I belatedly choked out, "Condom."

Tori's eyes widened slightly. I felt a jolt of relief to not be alone in the rushing force of our connection. My lips kicked up, my voice husky. "Almost forgot, but didn't."

After fetching a condom, I rolled it on in record time. I savored the way she slid down over me, sheathing me in her channel. Settling herself, she rocked her hips slightly, a tiny smile curling her lips. "There," she whispered.

I shifted back into the pillows. I felt the brush of her nipples against my chest as we began to rock together. My hand laced in her hair as her forehead fell to mine. With that familiar push and pull, the clenching of her core around me, everything spun tight inside. It felt like a storm gathering force.

Her name was a chant on my lips as I reached between us. I knew her body now, knew when she was chasing her release. She cried out, her voice ragged, as she came. Her pussy clamped more tightly, as she trembled around me and over me. My own release, *finally*, broke loose.

I held her tight and close, savoring the feel of her going soft against me as the storm abated. When she lifted her head a few moments later and her eyes locked with mine, the resounding thump of my heart was definitive. I knew I was in love with her.

I hadn't expected any of this.

I stared into Kincaid's eyes, lost in the blur. This moment felt startlingly intense and intimate. I knew I was in love with him, and it terrified me.

My body felt sated, as I always did, when I was with him. Meanwhile, my insecurity clamored, as if scrambling to make its voice known, to remind me of all the reasons I couldn't trust anyone. And yet, my body knew a different story. I knew that I felt safe with him.

His hand loosened in my hair, his touch sliding down in an easy pass along the center of my back to rest on my hip. "Tori." His voice was gruff.

My heart felt cracked wide open. I had to clear my throat. "Yeah?"

His lips twitched, just barely, at the corners. "I just wanted to say your name," he added before leaning forward and giving me a lingering kiss.

My mouth opened easily under his because, with him, I always wanted more. On the heels of that kiss, when I saw the flicker of something in his gaze, I wanted to comfort him. This was an unfamiliar feeling. When he leaned back slightly, I lifted my hand, trailing my fingertips, along his stubbled jaw. Kincaid was handsome, but when he had that five o'clock shadow, I just loved it.

I cupped his cheek lightly, my thumb tracing along his bottom lip. "Are you okay?" I asked.

His eyes widened slightly. "Of course, I'm okay. I'm more than okay, I mean—" He gestured between us. "It's always incredible when I'm with you."

All of a sudden, emotion rushed through me, like an unexpected fierce wind whipping something loose. It almost overwhelmed me, and I had to blink away the prick of tears.

"Hey, you okay?" he asked softly.

I cleared my throat, swallowing before I nodded. "Yeah," was all I could manage.

I fell asleep with him. Again. I loved falling asleep with Kincaid. I felt safe and protected. I loved waking up beside him, the way he was always warm, to my usual chilly. I savored his strong presence. Sometimes, if I let myself think about how I felt, he was like an island of calm for me.

The next morning, he teased me to yet another orgasm. He doled those out like candy when it came to me, handfuls of pure pleasure.

———

It was still early in the afternoon when he texted me to say he had to go out for a fire. I knew hotshot firefighters got called out unexpectedly, but still, my heart dipped for a second. On impulse, I stopped by the station to give him a kiss before he left. Solely because I wanted to, and I didn't even let myself think too hard about it.

Maisie gave me a warm, knowing look as I walked out. She was tied up on a call, so I just waved and went over to Firehouse Café. When I walked in, I was feeling good. Almost giddy. Almost like I'd finally silenced the doubts in my mind.

Unfortunately, Shelly was there. She was waiting in line ahead of me. For a heartbeat, I almost turned around and left, but then I realized I could either keep running from this or face it down and all that she represented to me—a bundle of betrayal and baggage I'd been lugging around while she tried to get me, my mom, and the whole freaking town to forgive her.

So I lifted my chin and braced myself inside. When I saw Casey behind the counter, she met my gaze and dipped her chin in the tiniest nod. Somehow, she gave me the burst of courage I needed.

After I ordered, I stopped beside Shelly, coffee in one hand and a pastry bag with my bagel and cream cheese gripped tightly in the other. "I'm guessing you want to talk. Let's talk," I said flatly.

In a way, it was a little assertive—maybe aggressive—but I didn't know how else to do this.

Shelly met my gaze. "I'd like that."

We sat down at a table in the corner. What hurt, as I looked over at her, was that I knew Shelly so well. She had babysat me so many times. Her daughter Michelle had been at my house as much as I'd been at hers. Shelly herself had been like family to me.

I took a deep breath, uncertain how to start. Just as I was fumbling, I realized it was really on her to start this conversation. I didn't owe her an apology for anything. I waited. My stomach was twisting nervously, and my heart was racing with anxiety and dread.

She was quiet for a few beats. I took a swallow of coffee, savoring the jolt of bitterness, as if it could fortify me.

"Look." She let out a breath. "I don't know how to make this right. I'm really sorry. I've told your mom I'm sorry. I've told Michelle I'm sorry. To this day, she hates me because, according to her, I ruined her hometown for her."

"Well, you ruined it for all of us," I added, because that was the truth. That was how I'd felt for years.

She blinked. Her voice dropped to barely above a whisper. "Has your mom talked to you about it?"

"Yeah. She told me you talked to her and that she's let it go."

Hope flared in Shelly's eyes. "You don't think just because she's let it go that she wants to be your friend again, do you? Because that would be insane, Shelly. You had an affair with my dad for ten years. That was years and years of lying. It was a huge betrayal."

"I know."

"I have to figure my own life out, but trust will probably be a lifelong issue for me, because my dad did something I never imagined him doing. You did something I never imagined you doing." I shrugged. "It was a lesson I never wanted to have to learn—that people aren't always who you think they are, even if and especially when you trust them."

Shelly's eyes were bright with tears, and she blinked quickly. "I know. I still don't know what I was thinking."

For the first time ever, I actually felt a flicker of sympathy for her, a feeling I never could have imagined having.

"Shelly... all of this is hard to sort through, because some of it I just can't imagine. If it had been a one-time thing, maybe I could chalk it up to a moment. But it went on for *years*. You and my dad lied and lied and lied."

"I know." She twisted a napkin between her fingers. "Look, I've even talked to a therapist about this. I just... I'm sorry. I really, really am. And I hope you can forgive me. I hope maybe we can rebuild something."

I held her gaze and shook my head slowly. "There are a lot of things that could happen, and I'm not sure if I'm at forgiveness yet. But I'm never going to trust you. That was such a selfish, long-term betrayal. For most of my childhood, the person I thought you were wasn't who you were. You were lying to all of us, and it tore my family apart. Obviously, I also hold my dad responsible, but it was a betrayal on both of your parts. I can't pretend that's not the case."

She sighed. "I know. I'm sure you know he cheated on me, too."

"Of course I do. I don't know why you thought he wouldn't."

"He also never got over your mom." There was bitterness in Shelly's words, and mostly, it just made me feel sad. "He turned out to be a very selfish man."

"Yeah, he did." I paused, taking a slow breath. "So you wanted to talk, and we talked," I finally said when the silence stretched between us. "Did you just want to talk for absolution, and the hope that I would just snap my fingers and... I don't know..." I shook my head. "I won't call us friends. You were like an aunt. A second mom to me."

She blinked and stayed quiet for a few beats. "I know. No, I guess I'm just too hopeful. Maybe."

I shrugged.

"I think for you to feel okay here, in this—" I gestured around us "—in the scene of the lies where everybody knows what happened, you're going to have to work a little harder than you're used to. You're going to have to get used to being accountable for what happened." Her face fell, but I kept going. "Why would anyone trust you as a friend? You're going to have to earn that. That still doesn't mean you're going to get it—with my mom or me."

Her shoulders rose and fell with a deep breath.

"How's Michelle?" I asked.

"She's okay. Still in Anchorage." She looked down at her coffee. "Maybe it'll make you feel better to know she was—and still is—furious with me. She hated that we moved away and that I married your dad. She told me I deserved it when he cheated on me."

I didn't even know what to say to that, so I said nothing.

"She says she misses being friends with you," Shelly added.

Michelle and I hadn't been best friends, but we had been close-ish. Sort of like siblings. She had practically lived at our house as much as I'd lived at hers. Her behavior toward me after it all came out hadn't been great. I had enough sense to recognize she was lashing out in her own way.

At the time, I felt like I'd gotten the short end of the stick. Like they had won my dad, and I'd been left behind in the wreckage. But sitting here now, I realized maybe that wasn't how it worked out over time. Michelle had been moved away from her home, from her friends.

"Well, she's welcome to reach out," I said.

Hope flared again in Shelly's eyes.

"You can give her my number. But it doesn't mean you're going to get whatever it is that you're hoping to get from my mom or me. We can't absolve you. Look, I'm not you. I haven't had an affair with my best friend's husband and blown a family apart. You're going to have to do the work of coming to terms with that yourself. When all is said and done, it doesn't mean you're going to get what you want." I paused before adding, "It's not going to go away. What happened *happened*."

Shelly nodded just as Janet stopped by the table, coffee pot in hand. She glanced between us. "How's it going, ladies?"

I met Janet's gaze, the warmth and understanding held there easing the anxiety racing through me in a loop of nervous energy. I was handling this better than I could've expected, but inside, I was rattled.

"It's okay," I said, knowing there was no sense in trying to gloss it over.

Shelly looked up at Janet, pain flickering in her eyes. "I really fucked up," she said bluntly.

Janet nodded. "This is not going to be easy."

"No, it's not," Shelly murmured before she asked, "Should I apologize to the whole town?"

Janet rolled her eyes. "Really, Shelly? Don't be so dramatic. No, you shouldn't apologize to the whole town. But the whole town knows. Or at least everybody who knew you and Tori's father. We all make mistakes, and we all have to live with the mistakes and the consequences that come with them."

Shelly nodded slowly. "I guess we do."

Janet met my eyes again. "You okay?"

"I'm fine. Really," I offered.

With a nod, she moved to another table.

Somehow, Shelly and I ended the conversation on a polite note. It felt, to me, that there was nothing left to add. After Shelly left, I sat there at the table for a while. I could even eat the bagel I'd gotten, which surprised me.

A few minutes later, Janet slid into the seat across from me. "How are you now, Tori?" she asked gently.

I snorted. "I'm actually okay. I've been putting off that conversation, or maybe avoiding it altogether. I don't think Shelly got what she wanted out of it, but I feel okay." I paused. "I actually feel a little bad for her."

Janet nodded. "I do too. She made this mess for herself. We all know your dad was part of it, but he's gone. She has to live with the repercussions on her own. I do believe she's sorry, but I don't think she's grasping how deep the betrayal was. It feels like she's hoping if she gets your mom back as a friend that she'll find her own absolution."

"Exactly."

# Chapter Twenty-One

# TORI

That evening, my conversation with Shelly spun through my thoughts. I was surprised to discover that I felt relieved. As my mother had suggested I might.

I'd built such a thick wall around my lingering hurt, just to keep myself from even acknowledging what had happened with her. Now that I had finally spoken with Shelly, I realized something—waiting that long had only dragged it out emotionally for me.

Impulsively, I called my mom.

"Hey, hey," she answered.

"I did it," I said by way of greeting.

I didn't have to explain further. My mom knew exactly what I was talking about. "Good for you. How do you feel?"

I paused, tilting my head to the side. "Better. I really do, and I kind of can't believe it."

I could hear the understanding in her voice as she replied, "I can believe it. I completely understand why it took you a while to get to the point where you were ready to hear her out. It isn't so much about giving her what she wants. It's about just letting yourself face it."

"I feel like I've been facing it ever since it all blew up," I pointed out.

"Oh, you have. But with her coming back like this and wanting something from you—and me and others—it was something you had to face. A different layer, I guess. How do you feel?" she repeated.

"Relieved, and sort of at peace." I paused and did a quick internal scan of myself. "I'm never going to be happy about what happened. For obvious reasons." My mother's laugh was dry. "But I feel okay. I feel like I can do what you suggested, which is to let it go. I know that I need to. Have you heard from Michelle?"

"I haven't." My mother's sigh filtered through the line. "I don't feel like it's my place to reach out to her. She was caught in the crossfire, too. If she ever reaches out to me, obviously, I'll talk to her."

"It sounds like things aren't great with her and Shelly," I said.

My mother was quiet for a beat. "It is what it is."

"It is," I said emphatically. "Thanks, Mom."

"For what?"

"For telling me it was worth having that conversation. Now I don't feel like I'm going to be angry every time I see her, and I needed that."

"Good. How's everything else?"

I paused, thinking about Kincaid and that twist in my heart whenever I did. That ache of missing him when he was away.

"They're good. I've, um, I've started seeing Kincaid."

"I know." My mother's tone was amused.

"What do you mean, you know?"

She outright laughed. "Exactly that. Of course I know. How big do you think this town is? Word travels. I'm happy for you. Janet tells me he's a good man."

"I think he is." I chewed on the side of my cheek, trying to ignore the anxiety that started to spin in my chest. "Mom?"

"Right here, hon."

"I don't know how to trust anybody." My eyes stung with the tears that wicked up from my throat suddenly.

The silence that followed felt heavy and loaded with so much. I could hear my mother take a breath and let it out in a gust. "I know," was all she said.

# Chapter Twenty-Two

# KINCAID

*A few days earlier*

I'd kind of blocked out that I was about to speak to my father for the first time in my life. I mostly agreed to talk to him because I knew how much my mom wanted me to.

Okay, *maybe* I was also curious. When you're a kid, and one parent is absent, you eventually understand that the one present is holding your life together with a little duct tape, some patchy glue, and a lot of love. It's the opposite of the parent who isn't there.

I trusted my mother completely, and I knew she had told my father of my existence. So I'd spent most of my life wondering why he never reached out. His existence was a giant question mark in my life, my mind, and my heart.

With my mom seated beside me at the kitchen table, her gaze was warm. "Okay, are you ready?" she asked.

I angled my head to the side, giving her a look. "Yeah, Mom. I'm ready as I'll ever be. Let's just do this." I bit back a sigh.

Within a minute, a man's voice came through the line.

"Hi, Claudia."

It felt like a ball of energy slammed into my solar plexus. I'd never even heard my father's voice.

"Hi, Mark, I have Kincaid here," my mom said.

My father went very quiet, but I could hear the sound of his breathing and tried to ignore the rattle in it. "Hi," he said simply.

"Hi. My mom wanted to call," I replied.

Although a buzzy energy was coursing through me and my fingertips were tingling from it, I could still speak, somehow. I figured I might as well be truthful about how this call came to be. My mom narrowed her eyes, pressing her lips together. I could see the disappointment contained in her gaze, but it was what it was. She was the one who had taught me about the importance of being honest.

My dad cleared his throat. He couldn't mask the fact that his breathing was labored, and he sounded, to be uncomfortably honest with myself, pretty sick. "I'm sure you think I'm an asshole, because I know your mom. Maybe I only knew her for a short time, but I have zero doubt that she's been—and is—an incredible mother to you."

My chest tightened, and I blinked away the sting of tears in my eyes. "She is."

"Do you have any questions for me?" he asked.

I paused, trying to gather my thoughts amidst the snarling mess of my emotions. "Aside from things about family history and so on, which Mom has kind of gotten for me, I guess I want to know why."

I hoped he knew what I meant because it was really going to suck if he didn't.

But he did. He let out a slow and heavy sigh. "Because I was young and stupid. And then, after I stopped being young and stupid, I was a coward. I wish I had some great explanation— something that made sense. If I'm being honest, which I am, I spent years trying to think of how I could reach out and how I could cover up my absence from your life. I completely let you down, and I completely let your mother down. That remains my deepest regret, and I will go to my grave with it."

His blunt truth slammed into me, almost freezing me for a

moment. I took a quiet breath, trying to steady myself as my mother jumped in.

"I appreciate your honesty, Mark. We did just fine on our own."

"Mom," I cut in. "Yeah, we did fine, but you barely squeaked by sometimes."

She pinned me with a look, and I could see the hint of disappointment there, but I wasn't as forgiving as her. "You can't see my mom's face, but she's pissed with me. She's nicer than me. I didn't have a dad, and I always wondered why. Well, I mean, I had one—*you*—but I do appreciate your honesty. I'm glad you agreed to finally talk to me. What's going on with your health?" I cut straight to the core with that question. I needed to know.

"I'm sick. I have a lung disease from exposure to something during my military time."

"It sounds uncomfortable," I pointed out.

"It is." I could practically feel his shrug through the phone line. "I'm okay. I mean, as okay as I can be."

"How long do you have to live?"

My mom gave me another look, and I ignored her. This wasn't all rainbows for me. I guess it was good. I wouldn't call this conversation closure because I didn't really believe in closure, but it offered me answers. It offered answers to so many questions that had lingered inside of me for so long.

"Six months, give or take. I don't expect you to want to meet me, and I can't travel," he said.

"We could do video calls," my mom chirped, her voice bright.

I rolled my eyes, but I humored her. "We could, Mom."

I heard Mark's chuckle. "It's up to you, Kincaid. I would actually love to see you before..." He cleared his throat roughly. "Whether it's video or in person, I'd love to see you before I pass. Not because I expect it to be easy. I know that I can't repair what happened. But I just want you to know I will die with this weighing heavily on me. I let you down, and I'm grateful your mom reached out again."

"Is this the first time she reached out?" I asked. I already knew the answer from my mother's perspective, but I needed to know how he'd answer this.

"No, it's not. I'm sure you know that. But again, that was cowardly of me."

This time, I cleared my throat. There seemed to be a surplus of that in this conversation. "I appreciate your honesty about everything. I think we could do a video call. I'm about to leave to go out to a fire, this afternoon, actually. I'll probably be out for a couple of weeks."

I glanced toward my mom. "I'm sure she'll set something up when I get back."

She beamed at me. Once again, I could hear the rattle in my father's breath when he chuckled. "I'm sure she will. It's good to hear your voice, Kincaid."

After that, we ended the call. I honestly don't remember how we said goodbye.

My mom was all misty-eyed across the kitchen table from me. She reached for both of my hands and held them in hers, squeezing hard. "I'm proud of you, honey."

My brows hitched slightly as I tilted my head to the side. "I know you're proud of me, Mom, and that's the only reason I was able to make this call. You have been and are the best mom anybody could ever ask for."

"Do you really mean it? Will you do a video call with him?" she pressed.

"I mean it, Mom." I squeezed her hands again. My heart ached a little. As close as I was with my mother, I wasn't ready to process this fully just yet. I needed time. It worked out that this happened the same day I found out we were traveling to a fire, which gave me some built-in time to think.

"Now I gotta go."

"I know, I know. Thank you for making that call before you left."

"You got it. Love you, Mom."

*Chapter Twenty-Three*

# KINCAID

*A week into the fire*

"Ah, hell," Graham muttered as he sat down, dragging his sleeve across his face.

I glanced sidelong toward him. "Yeah, that's one way to put it."

"This fire is an asshole," Hudson chimed in.

I barked a laugh just as Parker reached us. He set a chainsaw on the ground and sank onto the wide fallen log that Graham was already perched on. "You found the only tree," Parker said.

Graham glanced down at the charred hunk of tree he was seated on. "Well, most of them have been burned," he pointed out dryly.

Within the hour, the rest of our crew had gathered. This was officially a safe zone now, because there was nothing left to burn, no fuel left for the fire. Nothing of worth anyway. Fire has to have fuel to keep burning.

We'd been out here with another crew from Willow Brook, along with a crew from Fairbanks, fighting a massive wildfire in the interior of Alaska. Just like most of the West, fires were becoming more common because summers were hotter and winters weren't as cold.

"How much longer do you think we're gonna be out here?" I asked Graham, who was the superintendent for our crew.

He let out a breath. "Maybe a week. We've got this section under control. The Fairbanks crews are gonna move around to the other side, and we'll stay over here to establish safety lines. The river a few miles away gives us a natural barrier, and apparently, some rain should be rolling in within the next few days. After that, we head back."

That evening, we actually got to relax a little more than we had so far. When fighting wildfires, we had a lot of gear to carry. The work was grueling. We ate light and slept light until the fire was enough under control that we could relax a bit.

Tonight, we played cards, traded jokes, and gradually spread out to sleep. I lay awake for a little while, staring up at the sky, which felt so vast here in Alaska. There was zero light pollution out here. The nearest town was over one hundred miles away. It felt like I could stretch a fingertip up and touch the stars.

Tori sashayed into my thoughts. I missed her. Fuck, I missed her. That was a new feeling for me. I thought about my mom's hopefulness—for me to have a relationship, to build something lasting.

A fuzzy, gray emotion floated through me. I didn't know how else to describe it. It wasn't black or bitter, not resigned or angry either. That used to be how I felt about my dad. But those old feelings were sort of neutralized a little. Maybe.

If he hadn't been so honest, I wasn't sure I would've believed a word he said. But he had acknowledged the reality, and that mattered. Honesty was something my mom had drilled into me from the start. Tell the truth. Own your choices. I trusted people more when they admitted they'd screwed up.

With my dad, ignoring my existence was a pretty damn big screw-up. I did a quiet check-in with myself—plumbing the emotional depths of that little boy still inside me. The one who had grown up without a dad. The one who'd still hoped to meet him for so many years. Now, somehow, I'd finally connected with him. Less than a year before he was probably going to leave this earth.

It was a strange relief. Not that he was sick and facing down the end of his life. At least, I didn't have to wonder anymore. I had the truth. I could sit there and tell myself I would've handled things differently if I'd been in his shoes. Maybe I would have. But he and my mom were barely more than teenagers. She had been twenty-two when she got pregnant. She'd joined the Air Force straight out of high school.

I was thirty-three now. The idea of being a parent felt like a big deal. When I'd been the age my mother was when she had me, I couldn't imagine what that must've been like. Contemplating the responsibility of a having a child would've terrified me.

I took a long, slow breath and let it out. Tori slipped into my thoughts again, nudging her way inside the way she always did— quietly, insistently. She was the first woman I'd been with where I actually wondered about the future.

Oh, hell. I *knew* I wanted more with her. I didn't even like considering the thought of not seeing her when I got back. That had never even occurred to me before when I'd even casually dated.

I'd always figured I was the perfect fit for this kind of life, for being a hotshot firefighter. No ties. No missing someone I loved when I was out in the field.

But now? I was surrounded by men on my crew who were happily committed. Many of them had kids back home. They made it work.

In the end, if I'd learned anything from my mom, it was that you made the life you had work. She had done more than that with me.

I knew that no matter what happened with Tori, we could make it work, too. But I also knew how hard trust came for her, and the long shadows cast by what happened in her family.

I understood why. What a fucking asshole her dad had been.

I took another deep breath, letting it out slowly as I stared up at the stars. I counted a few and tried to get my thoughts settled before I drifted off to sleep.

# Chapter Twenty-Four

# TORI

*Two weeks later*

"They got extended," Maisie said, shaking her head slightly. "Sometimes they're out for as long as a month." I'd just stopped by Firehouse Café and encountered Maisie there at the counter.

"I heard they haven't gotten any rain up there yet either," I added. I took a swallow of coffee, willing the churn of my anxiety to slow inside. I missed Kincaid, and I didn't even know what to do with that feeling.

"I miss Beck," Maisie said flatly.

Casey tipped her head to the side. "Completely understand. I always miss Leo when he's out working."

All of a sudden, Maisie turned toward me. "Do you miss Kincaid?"

My cheeks burned. I tried to play it cool before I gave up and let out a little laugh. "Yes, I do. In all honesty, I miss him a lot."

"It's not great, but you'll get used to it," she offered matter-of-factly.

"Will I, though?" I couldn't help but ask.

Casey sighed. "You'll have to if you're going to stay with him. If you don't want to get used to it, well, you'd better stay away from the firefighters."

I snorted. "There's a lot of firefighters in Willow Brook."

"Tell me about it," Luna said dryly.

"How serious are you two?" Casey asked.

I paused, contemplating that question, as much for myself as for trying to answer. "I don't know," I said slowly.

"What do you mean you don't know?" Maisie asked, her brows rising.

"I don't know," was all I could offer in return. I wished I knew how serious we were. I knew my feelings were starting to feel big in a way I'd never expected. Against my better judgment, Kincaid had knocked away my defenses, and I hadn't even seen him coming.

Just then, a cluster of customers came in, and Casey and Luna shifted into work mode to wait on them. Maisie dragged me over to a table. "I need company—adult company," she explained as we sat down.

My brows hitched up. "Adult company?"

"Well, yes. I spent the whole morning with the kids. Beck is so good when he's here. He helps a lot with the kids. So when he's gone..." She shrugged. "I love being a mom, but sometimes talking to children under the age of six for hours on end makes me desperate to talk to adults." She straightened in her chair, her eyes brightening. "Tell me about you and Kincaid. We can clarify just how serious you are. I'm here for you."

"Maisie," I sputtered. "I don't know. Plus, I have trust issues."

Just then, the bell above the door jingled, and I glanced over. For a moment, I wondered where I'd seen the woman who came in. In a flash, I remembered.

"What? Who's that?" Maisie asked.

"Oh, my gosh. I waited on that woman a while ago. She was here on a divorce trip because, well, she got divorced. She had some friends with her. They were a fun group and left me a huge tip. I don't remember her name, though."

I shifted my focus back to Maisie. "Anyway, I have trust issues. You heard the whole story about what happened with my parents. I'll figure it out, but I'm not ready to say I'm serious with Kincaid yet."

"But what if you *are* serious and your trust issues are just getting in the way of you acknowledging your feelings?" Maisie said, completely serious.

"Maisie!" She was so spot on, I shifted restlessly in my chair, feeling a little defensive.

"She's not wrong," a voice said from the table beside us.

We both glanced over together. The woman sitting there smiled. "Sorry, our tables are so close, I couldn't help but overhear. I'm a psychic."

"Really?" Maisie replied, completely focused on her now.

"Yes. I just moved to Willow Brook from Anchorage. I wanted to be in a smaller town." She gestured around the café with her hand. She was an older woman with wispy silver hair and twinkling brown eyes.

"I hope you like it here," Maisie said. "So, can you tell us her fortune? Are her and Kincaid going to fall in love and live happily ever after?"

"Maisie!" I protested again.

She giggled. "What's the harm in asking? You might as well find out. It might help with your trust issues."

Before I knew what was happening, this woman was seated at the table with us, reading my palm. She explained that I would have one child with a man I currently knew. "That's all I can see. I can't see more, and I can't see which man."

"My guess is it's Kincaid," Maisie cut in with authority.

"Oh, my God," I murmured with a sigh. Although I told myself not to take this too seriously, my little heart clapped with hope.

———

*Later that week*

. . .

I stared at the blue line. There were two of them, actually.

"I can't be pregnant. We used condoms," I said out loud, all by myself in my bathroom. I was sitting on the toilet. Because, I suppose, that's where one sat for this kind of news. "Oh, my God," my voice fell to a whisper. My mind zoomed back to the woman who read my palm and predicted I'd have one child with a man I already knew. I gasped.

Bella appeared in the doorway, nudging her head against my knees, while I was still staring at the pregnancy test in disbelief. When she lightly bumped my knee again, I glanced down, meeting her worried gaze. Even if her brown eyes were cloudy these days, I felt like I could still see her heart in them. No matter what, the love I felt from her grounded me.

"It's going to be fine," I told her.

She rubbed her head back and forth against my knee. Even though emotion was rising in a sharp crescendo inside me with tears stinging my throat and eyes, I laughed softly and reached to scratch behind her ears. I took several deep breaths.

"I don't know what to do," I said, still speaking out loud, my voice bouncing off the walls.

Another nudge on my knee from Bella. I scratched behind her ears again.

"What should I do?" I asked her.

She peered up at me, nothing but love radiating from her graying, loyal face. Her little half-tail wagged slowly back and forth, like she already knew the answer and was just waiting for me to catch up. I desperately wished Kincaid was back home.

And yet, I didn't even know if I was ready to tell him this.

"We used birth control," I murmured again, weakly, as if I could try to logic myself out of what I already knew.

I tried to replay our encounters in my head, but they were all a blur. I knew there had to have been one or two points where he teased his thick crown through my folds before he filled me and before he remembered to put the condom on. Hell, if it had been my job to put a condom on, I couldn't say I would have remembered.

"I can't have a baby," I announced to myself, idly stroking my fingertips through the soft hair along Bella's back.

I didn't know what I was going to do. And, I *really* didn't know what I was going to tell Kincaid.

"Oh my God," I murmured again.

*Four days later*

"Come on back," Maisie said, gesturing for me to follow her.

I trailed her down the hallway at the fire station into the back area, glancing around curiously. There was a locker room and a glimpse of showers through a door to one side. The hallway opened up to an area with a kitchen and a large table, a glassed-in workout room, and a lounging area with a large sectional and a flat screen TV mounted on the wall.

"It's nice back here," I commented.

Maisie tossed a grin over her shoulder, her dark curls bouncing in her ponytail. "They try to make it comfortable. Guys will sleep here sometimes, but not officially. Even the local crew, mostly they just respond when they're paged."

"How much longer until they get here?" I asked.

We walked through the back door and stepped into the sunshine, where I discovered a small cluster of friends already waiting. Madison, Tish, Stella, Luna, and Casey were all gathered as Maisie and I approached. "Wow. It's a party."

"It's been almost a month," Casey said with a dramatic sigh.

"I knew what I was signing up for, but damn, it's inconvenient to be in love with a firefighter. Especially a hotshot."

Maisie nodded. "You do get used to it." She paused, tapping her fingertips on her chin. "I think the absence—okay, I'm not trying to be cheesy—doesn't exactly make the heart grow fonder, but it definitely gives you more gratitude when they're home. You learn to savor every moment." She rolled her eyes. "Okay, that was a little cheesy."

Just then, the distant thrum of a helicopter reached us. A few minutes later, it landed, sending up a swirl of dust in the wind created by the propellers. Firefighters spilled out, hefting heavy gear as they stepped into the parking area.

I had one arm curled around my waist and the other nervously fiddling with the neck of my T-shirt. I was impatient. I wanted to see Kincaid. For the first time in days, I didn't obsess over the news I hadn't yet shared with anyone other than my dog.

When he finally climbed out of the aircraft, he was laughing at something Leo said. But the moment Leo spotted Casey and peeled off, Kincaid's attention shifted, his gaze arcing around.

His eyes locked on mine, and my heart flipped in my chest, slamming against my ribs as if clapping in joy. I didn't even realize I'd started running until he was moving toward me with long, purposeful strides. He met me halfway and pulled me into a strong, fast hug.

"Hey, sweetheart," he murmured, his hand cupping the back of my head, holding me tight.

My throat closed with emotion. I could feel the press of tears threatening, but I forced myself to take a few long breaths—breathing him in, grounding myself—before I stepped back.

"Hey," I said softly. "I missed you." Well, that was more direct than I'd intended.

He tipped his head slightly, a slow smile unfurling across his face. "I missed you, too. I probably smell like smoke and dirt."

"You definitely smell like smoke and dirt," Beck said dryly as he walked past, one arm slung around Maisie's shoulders and a backpack over his other shoulder.

Kincaid chuckled. "Yeah, I do. Let me grab my bag."

There were jokes and quips being tossed around as everyone made their way into the station. Once we were in the hallway, he caught my hand and walked beside me.

"Should I shower here?" he asked.

"What would you usually do?" I returned, trying not to care. Honestly, I didn't. I didn't care that he smelled like smoke and dirt . I was just glad he was back.

"I'd shower here."

"Well, then go for it."

"All right. Give me ten minutes. I'll meet you out back," he replied.

"I have Bella with me. I'll take her out for a pee break."

Bella was ecstatic to see Kincaid a little while later, wiggling and spinning in clumsy circles at his feet. He knelt to greet her, stroking his hands gently over her ears and pressing a kiss to her forehead.

"Good to see you, sweet girl," he said as he stood, grinning at me. "Dogs are the best."

"Dogs *are* the best," I agreed. "And, Bella in particular is the *very* best." I meant every word.

When he climbed into the car beside me and I started driving, I felt fragile in a way I hadn't expected. Maybe because I'd missed him more than I realized. Maybe because I had half-admitted to myself that I was falling in love with him. And maybe because the secret I carried inside me felt huge. I had already surprised myself with the decision I'd made.

I wanted this baby. It was so unexpected. If you had asked me before it happened—before I saw those two blue lines—if I would have made this decision, I would have said absolutely not. I one hundred percent would have chosen to have an abortion, hypothetically speaking.

While I would always be in support of a woman's right to

make her own choices about having a baby, my heart wanted something else in this moment. My heart wanted this baby. Wrapped up inside that wish was wanting this baby *with* Kincaid.

I was terrified. Because I didn't know what he wanted.

"How was the job, I guess?" I asked, my voice a little too bright and hitching on what to call his travel away.

Kincaid reached over, catching my hand where it rested on the center console, and laced his fingers through mine. He gave a warm squeeze. "Well, the fire's out."

A laugh slipped out. "That's the whole point, right?"

When I slid my gaze to his and caught the teasing glint in his eyes, my belly fluttered with a rush of nerves and anticipation.

"That is the point," he said, grinning. "But it's not always what happens, actually. Sometimes we go in for a rotation, get one section under control, and then roll out when another crew tags in. In this case, we got it close enough to one hundred percent containment on our side—with crews from Fairbanks on the other—that they kept us out longer to finish the job."

"Well, good." I smiled, stealing a longer glance at him. "Do you like your job?" I asked, genuinely curious.

Obviously, I knew the basics of what being a hotshot firefighter meant. We'd talked about it here and there, but not really in detail.

He paused for a beat. "Yeah, I do," he answered. "I got into it because I like being outdoors, and it seemed like a good way to do that." He shrugged, and I could feel the motion rather than see it since I was driving. "Sometimes I wonder if I should keep doing it long-term, especially with my mom's health. But she keeps insisting she doesn't need me to stay home all the time."

"I think you just do what works for you for the time being," I offered. "If at some point she does need you, I know you'll be there." I glanced over at him again. "I know this about you."

It should have surprised me that I trusted him that way. That I knew, without any doubts, that I could trust him to take care of his mom, that I trusted his loyalty. And yet, when it came to me—to *us*—I couldn't find the same confidence. I couldn't quite believe in the connection. I couldn't trust that anyone would really be there for me the way he tried to be there for his mom.

"That's pretty much how I've tried to think about it," he said.

Quiet settled between us, and I could hear the beat of my heart kicking along inside my chest.

"I missed you, Tori," he said softly.

I glanced at him, and my heart felt cracked wide open—emotion flooding in so fast it made my chest ache. I dragged my gaze back to the road.

"I missed you, too," I managed, my throat tight with emotion.

He gave my hand another slow squeeze.

I looked back toward him, meeting that rich brown gaze for half a heartbeat before I started to turn ahead.

"Moose!" he exclaimed.

I slammed my foot on the brakes. My attention jerked forward just in time to see a massive bull moose sauntering across the road ahead of us. We both watched in silence as the animal took its time—one slow step after another—before it paused at the edge of the trees to nibble on some alder.

"Take your time," I muttered under my breath.

"Rude," Kincaid teased, his chuckle rumbling across my nerves, which were already strung tight.

"I always wonder if it's impolite to honk at moose," I said.

"Probably not," he offered dryly.

I gave the horn a gentle tap. The moose lifted its head, his antlers swinging toward us with majestic disinterest. He eyed us for a long moment and then—without any actual movement that resembled a shrug—definitely seemed to shrug before disappearing into the trees.

I eased the car forward again. When we got back to my

house, Bella immediately curled up in her bed and fell asleep after a bathroom break in the yard.

I suddenly felt unaccountably nervous. Kincaid and I weren't brand new to each other anymore, but we were still new in our connection. He'd been gone for almost a month.

Everything felt fresh again. Like the next step might be one we couldn't take back.

I stood there uncertainly, looking over at him. He caught my hand and reeled me close, palming a cheek as he looked down into my eyes. "I missed you," he whispered, just before he claimed my mouth with a kiss.

It started slow, and then we were tumbling into the fire that was so intoxicating. Our clothes came off in a messy rush, and he bent me over the kitchen counter, his palms sliding down over my bottom as he murmured, "I missed you, sweetheart."

When I heard the familiar sound of him rolling a condom on, it was all I could do not to tell him there was no point. But I kept that thought silent, and let out a soft sigh of relief as he filled me in a slow surge. My release was already threatening, like lightning cracking across the sky before a storm. With each time he filled me, I heard myself panting his name before he reached around and teased me exactly where I needed it.

On the heels of that, I was crying out and shuddering, savoring the sharp pleasure and the sound of him saying my name in a ragged voice as he jerked against me.

# Chapter Twenty-Six

# KINCAID

We stumbled into the shower together. After we changed into comfortable clothes, we relaxed on the couch. Tori ordered pizza for delivery and made us both mugs of hot cocoa. I called my mom to check in and told her I'd be home tomorrow.

I could hear the smile in her voice when she said, "Well, I'm glad you're with Tori."

I just shook my head, biting back the urge to tell her to ease up on her hopes for my relationship. "See you tomorrow, Mom."

That night, falling asleep with Tori curled soft and warm against me was heaven. During our time out in the wilderness, some of the guys talked about how being gone made you really feel the absence of the people who mattered. I understood that now on a bone-deep level.

My fingers sifted slowly through her hair, and I savored the soft gust of her steady breath against my skin, where her head rested on my shoulder.

Into the darkness, I mouthed the words, *I love you.*

Over the following days, I spent every night with Tori. That wasn't our usual rhythm. Before, it had been every third night, sometimes less. It had felt unspoken, like a quiet agreement. But this time, we didn't talk about it. I just stayed with her. Night after night after night.

Maybe it wasn't a decision. Maybe we both just needed more. As good as it felt—and it *did* feel good—I sensed a subtle barrier between us. Not big, or dramatic. Just a tiny divide neither of us was quite ready to cross. I told myself it was because we were both feeling a lot. Maybe too much.

I also talked to my father again. A video call, this time. He looked tired, and frankly, sick. He looked surprisingly like me, only older, with grayer hair and a hollow look around his eyes. He looked like the kind of tired that seeps into the bones.

Even though I was braced for disappointment, for blame, for him to say something that would crack the fragile bridge we were building, he didn't. He owned his responsibility for what he hadn't been to me. Paradoxically, that made me a little angry.

Because if he was adult enough now to own what he'd done, to say it was his fault, then he'd been adult enough to do that years ago. Yet, he hadn't.

"You can't change the past," my mom kept reminding me.

Every time I spoke with him, she was more at peace. She seemed steady in a way that only time and distance, and lived experience could offer. Maybe it was age, or maybe it was just wisdom.

On maybe more than a whim, I decided to go visit him for a weekend. I didn't want to be away from Tori, but something in me was telling me I needed to go. I knew the time for me to actually meet him face to face had an end date. Maybe that date wasn't certain, but it was close.

When I told Tori about visiting him, she angled her head to the side and nodded slowly. "You need to, Kincaid. Not because I think you should," she said, her voice quiet. "But because that's how it feels for you. You're not going to have forever."

I watched her as she spoke, sensing the emotion flickering in her eyes. "I'm the first to say," she continued, "I think everybody has to stumble their way through things like this. I was so angry with my father for a long time. I still am in some ways. Things could have gone very differently. I honestly wish, in hindsight, I'd had at least a less stilted connection with him at the end. But I didn't, and I can't change that because he's gone now." She exhaled. "I've known people who find peace without reconnecting, and others who find peace by building a bridge, even when it's a messy situation. But no matter what, there's a clock ticking, so you kind of have to face what choice you feel you need to make."

"I know," I said gruffly.

I pulled her into a hug, holding her close. Because no matter what was coming next, I didn't want to let her go either.

# Chapter Twenty-Seven

# TORI

I needed to tell Kincaid I was pregnant. After my initial burst of confidence—an unexpected certainty that I wanted to have a baby—I started to doubt myself with questions ping-ponging around my brain for hours on end. All the while, a clock was ticking.

In the muddle of it all, I went to see my doctor. "How far along do you think I am?" I asked.

She tipped her head to the side, her gaze studying me for a beat. "Just over eight weeks. You caught it early because you missed your period."

"I know. If I didn't have such a regular cycle, I probably wouldn't have even taken a pregnancy test." I took a shaky breath.

"Do you know what you want to do?" she asked gently.

"I don't." I paused before I added quietly, "Actually, I think I do."

"Do you know who the father is?"

There wasn't even an ounce of judgment in her voice, which was the only reason I could answer with my heart jammed up in my throat. "Uh-huh. I need to tell him."

The words for how I'd tell Kincaid tumbled through my

thoughts all the next day. I needed to talk to him. And yet, this whole situation was dragging all my trust issues up to the surface. It felt like I had hundreds of emotional alarms sounding in this situation.

"Kincaid's a good man," I murmured to myself as I drove to work that evening.

"Yeah? And you thought your dad was a good man, too. Look how that worked out."

Good grief, I was to the point of two-way conversations with myself.

And yet, when it came to believing in my dad, it certainly hadn't just been me. Most of the town had considered him beyond reproach—a family man, loyal, reliable, the kind of guy you called when you needed help for anything from an actual emergency to shoveling your steps in a pinch.

I shook my head, blinking back the tears stinging my eyes. At least, I was still relieved I'd gotten up the nerve to talk to Shelly. I wouldn't say I had laid it all to rest. I didn't believe that's how things like that worked. Closure? Not a thing. You couldn't undo things.

There were different kinds of grief. When all was said and done, you had to live with the past, all of it. That was the getting-over part—learning how to keep moving and carry any scars from life with grace.

Though my father hadn't passed away until years after he'd detonated my trust, I'd still had to grieve him. I'd grieved the idea of him, the man I thought he was. I'd had to live with the betrayal I never saw coming. Those scars had healed over, but they were carved on my heart. My trust issues felt insurmountable sometimes.

"But Kincaid's a good man," I repeated to myself.

I took a deep breath and shook my head firmly. I needed to work. While it wasn't my goal to be a waitress forever, I actually enjoyed it. Plus, the pay was pretty good, especially now that tourist season was heating up.

Once I arrived at Fireweed Winery, I could mostly forget about Kincaid and the fact that I was pregnant. I was leaning toward keeping the baby, and yet, I hadn't spoken to anyone about this except my doctor.

Tish was floating around the restaurant tonight. As my shift was winding down, I spotted her at the table in the break room with David, who lived in Fireweed Harbor but seemed to spend most of his time here in Willow Brook these days. "What are you two doing now?" I teased lightly as I stopped beside them.

David grinned. "Specials. Can't get enough of them, you know?"

"No," I replied with a little eye-roll.

"Have you tried that mixed berry mead?" Tish asked, waggling her eyebrows.

I shook my head. "Not yet."

"You should have some now," she said.

David nudged an empty glass toward me, tapping the bottle beside it with one hand.

I shook my head again. "I'll pass. I'm tired tonight. I don't need anything to drink."

I saw the flicker of curiosity in Tish's gaze, but I ignored it. Not that I drank much anyway, but she knew how much I loved anything with berries.

Someone called for David from the kitchen, and he stood with a quick wink. "I'm sure I'll see you around, Tori."

When he walked off, Tish was still smiling at me. "What is it?" I asked.

She shrugged. "Nothing."

"Are we thinking big thoughts tonight?" I teased.

She laughed softly before her gaze sobered. "You know, when I moved here, I was in kind of a panic. I was pregnant and all alone. The father was ignoring me, and I didn't know what to do. Now, I feel like I belong here," Tish continued. "To be honest, that's not something I've experienced much in my life."

"What do you mean the father was ignoring you? Griffin's really involved," I pointed out.

Tish shook her head quickly. "Not Griffin. He adopted Teddy." She rolled her eyes. "I'm referring to Teddy's sperm donor before Griffin and I got serious." When my brows hitched up in question, she added, "We were dating, but he ghosted me before I found out I was pregnant." She shook her head, as if to herself. "I was so stupid."

"What do you mean?"

"Unplanned pregnancies and all that." She gave a wry smile.

My words slipped out without any thought. "Tell me about it."

Her eyes narrowed slightly. "What do you mean?"

I wanted to play it off, but the need to talk to someone overrode everything else. With a blush heating my cheeks. I sat down with a thump in the chair across from Tish. "I'm pregnant. And, I'm *completely* freaking out."

Tish immediately reached for both of my hands, curling hers around them and holding firm. Her grip was warm and steady, and I could feel the strength she was trying to lend me.

I blinked rapidly, trying to hold myself together, but my tears spilled over anyway. "If you didn't know, birth control doesn't always work," I whispered.

She released one of my hands, snagged the box of tissues in the center of the table, and thrust it toward me. I took a handful, dabbing at my eyes and blowing my nose. "Yeah. So, uh, we used birth control, and I'm pregnant anyway."

"It happens. I'm assuming Kincaid is the father?" she asked hesitantly.

I nodded slowly. "The only possibility."

"Does he know?"

"Now *that's* a loaded question, Tish," I said dryly before I shook my head. I took in a deep breath and let it out slowly. "I *know* I need to talk to him. But first I have to decide what I'm going to do."

She held my gaze for a few beats. "Look, if you decide to have the baby, yes, you need to tell him. But until you make that call, what you do is your choice."

Her tone was calm and practical and slightly eased the anxiety churning inside of me. "I know. I'm about ninety-eight percent sure I want to have the baby." I shook my head slowly, rolling my eyes as I lifted my hands and let them fall into my lap. "I'm still almost dismayed that I'm even contemplating this. If you had told me—frankly, minutes before I saw that positive pregnancy test—that I would want to keep a baby I didn't plan to have? I would've told you no way. No how. Never, never, never. And yet..." I trailed off. "Here I am seriously thinking about it, and I can't even believe it."

"It's okay," she assured me gently.

"I know it's okay, but what the hell am I thinking?" I muttered.

Tish tilted her head to the side, her gaze kind and understanding. "Honestly? I could've said any of the things you're saying right now when I found out I was pregnant. In my case, it was a little more complicated because we started with a condom, and he stealthed me."

My mouth dropped open. "Oh, my God. Are you serious?"

She nodded. "Oh yeah. It's a crime in some states now. Not here in Alaska yet, though."

"Oh, my God," I whispered.

"Anyway," she went on, "it all worked out for the best. I didn't plan it. He wanted nothing to do with Teddy. Pretty much blew me off the whole time." She smiled softly. "And then, Griffin and I fell in love. It hasn't been the easiest—we still had to jump through a few legal hoops because the sperm donor's kind of a jerk. But I'm here to tell you: no matter what you do—and I don't have an opinion about what you do—I seriously considered abortion, too. But I decided against it." She shrugged. "Even though, logically, it probably wasn't the easy choice. You just have to do what feels right for you. What is it?" she asked, as more tears spilled over my cheeks.

Just when I thought I had them under control. "I just... I don't know what to do. Obviously, Kincaid didn't plan on having a baby, because we did use birth control. I don't know." I swallowed hard. "What if it doesn't work out with him? This is terrifying for me. He seems like a good man."

"I think he is," she added.

"I don't—" My voice wavered. "I have major trust issues. Because of what happened with my dad."

"Yeah," I said softly, "like the whole freaking town trusted that man. Everyone."

"Well, maybe not everyone," Tish replied, giving me a look. "But lots of people were surprised, from what I understand. It doesn't mean what he did is something most people would do. Maybe if you're ninety-eight percent sure you're going to have this baby, you should talk to Kincaid about it."

I opened my mouth to reply, but she held up a hand. "Maybe you just tell him all your worries. Tell him that you're not sure you can trust him—but that it's not him. It's trusting anyone."

"Tish," I protested. "You make it sound like that's simple."

"Oh, it's definitely not simple," she said, laughing under her breath. "Few things are." She paused before circling her hand in the air. "But when I got pregnant, it clarified everything for me. At least it did once I accepted it. It was like all these things I used to wonder about, or worry about, I could suddenly assess them quickly. This is right. This is what I want. This isn't. That kind of thing. My priority was my baby, and it made other things easier to not worry about, if that makes any sense."

I exhaled slowly, feeling that pressure in my chest build again.

"I can't tell you what to do," she said. "But I'm here if you want to talk more. Call any time. I've never been the best sleeper, so even if you're up in the middle of the night—just send me a text. I'll wake up and listen as long as you need."

My eyes went wide as I let out a disbelieving laugh. "Are you serious?"

"Absolutely. Although I'm making it sound like it was easy for me to decide to have Teddy, it wasn't. Not at the time." She leaned back, her expression softening. "It's true that everything felt clearer once I made the decision, and especially after he came into my life. But I felt so alone through it all at first. I really did. Honestly, moving here helped me. I love my job. You know Phoebe?"

I nodded. "Yeah. We both grew up here."

"She and Archer have that little garage apartment behind their place. I ended up renting it from them for a bit. Phoebe helped me so much. She still does. After that, I moved into the place Madison rents to us now." Her lips curled slightly with a smile. "She's another good friend. I don't think you have to have a lot of friends in this life. But I feel lucky because I have more than I ever imagined here. It's the good ones who matter."

I swallowed hard. My throat was suddenly tight, and I blinked against the sting behind my eyes.

"You don't have to be anything other than yourself for those kind of friends," she added softly.

Holding her gaze, I reached for her hands, squeezing them firmly before letting go. "You're a good friend, Tish."

Her eyes warmed. "Ditto." She sat back and looked toward the window. "When do you see Kincaid again?"

"He actually flew down to Seattle this weekend to see his dad. He and his mom went down there."

Tish nodded slowly. "So... when he gets back? You could try to talk to him about what's going on. Handling it all by yourself will only make it more difficult."

I sighed. "I know you're right. I have to talk to him."

"The world won't end if you don't," she said, lifting one shoulder in a shrug. "But if he's important to you—which I sense he is—you have to talk to him."

———

When I got home that night, I walked Bella out into the yard. An owl hooted at us from the trees nearby. I wasn't even sure Bella could hear the sound. The sky was dark with the moon rising above the mountains.

I took a deep breath, savoring the crisp, fresh air. Bella seemed to sense that I needed her presence, and she lingered close beside me as we walked back inside. I sank onto the couch, and she curled up next to me, resting her head in the curve of my hip as I idly stroked over her ears—her favorite way to be petted. That slow, steady breathing of hers and the warmth of her fur beneath my fingers soothed something raw inside of me.

"I have to talk to him, Bella," I whispered as I glanced down.

Her trusting, cloudy gaze met mine, her little tail wagging. Even though I wasn't sure how to do this, I knew that she had faith in me.

# Chapter Twenty-Eight

# KINCAID

My actual father sat across from me at a table. This entire situation was both odd and oddly comfortable. My mom had come with me at the start, and they'd hugged—which was also odd. She had just gone out to pick up a pizza for us for lunch. He'd said that was one of the few things he still had an appetite for.

His hair was thin and his eyes were tired. There was no other way to describe his face except haggard and weathered. It was clear the man had lived a life. But he'd been in the Air Force for most of his life and spent much of that career deployed overseas. We'd gotten through, as he put it, the "speed-dating summary" of his life.

"I'm really grateful you came to meet me." His voice was low and a little worn.

"Yeah." I paused, taking measure of how I felt inside my body. "I'm glad I came too. Which, to be honest, surprises me."

He tilted his head to the side. "That doesn't surprise me."

"No?"

"I wasn't there when you were growing up, and I regret it. Your mom raised an amazing man."

"She's the best," I said, my chest tightening with emotion.

"She seems pretty awesome."

I chuckled. "Well, you dated her once upon a time."

He nodded. "I did. I don't know what you were like when you were twenty-four, but even though I was technically an adult, I was, to put it lightly, emotionally immature. Of course, I didn't know it at the time. I liked your mom a lot. She was cute and smart and funny. But I was too young to know what I needed to grab ahold of at that time. I'd like to think, if I'd found out about her being pregnant before I was transferred, that I would have handled it differently. But I don't know. I was young and carefree. I've had to accept my mistakes, and it kind of sucks."

His directness elicited a startled laugh from me. "Is that so?"

"Yeah." His chin bobbed. "Totally sucks. There are some things you can do over in life, but there are some things you can't. Your mom has shown me plenty of pictures. Hell, last week, she sent me online folders of photos labeled for every year of your life." He shook his head, his eyes bright with a sheen. "I wish I'd been there. So, I wouldn't give you the advice to live your life the way I chose to live mine. By the way, I never got married and never had any other kids."

I was quiet and still, feeling the weight of his words sinking in. "I wondered, so thanks for letting me know." Pausing, I gathered myself. "I'm glad you took my mom's call," I finally added.

"I'm more glad than I can say," he said quietly.

Time rolled along, and we shifted from the heavier topics to more casual conversation, which was a relief. If anything, because I appreciated that we both felt relaxed enough to talk casually. By the time my mom and I left to return to the hotel, I felt lighter inside. So many questions had been answered. More than anything, I felt like I finally knew the man my father was. That was a gift I would cherish.

The following morning, we had breakfast together. When we

flew home, all I could think about was Tori. I needed to tell her how I felt. I needed not to let what we had slip away. No matter what happened with us, I was at least going to put my feelings out there so she knew.

# Chapter Twenty-Nine

# TORI

Bella started spinning in her happy circles as soon as Kincaid walked into the house. He gave me a quick kiss before leaning down to greet her. "Hey, sweet girl," he murmured, and her little tail quivered in joy.

Maybe some people would've felt slighted that he initially gave my dog more attention than me, but it only solidified what a good man he was for me. That little voice of doubt, that deep distrust in the world and in my ability to understand what a person could be capable of, chimed in, *Dad loved dogs too*.

*Oh, shut up*, I muttered silently to myself.

Kincaid straightened, and Bella meandered off to her bed. He stood in front of me, his gaze skating over my face for a few beats. "Missed you, Tori," he murmured as he pulled me into an embrace.

I took the moment to breathe him in, to absorb his presence. "I missed you too," I murmured into the curve of his shoulder.

His fingers idly sifted through my hair, and when I lifted my head to peer up at him, my chest was tight with so many unspoken emotions and, well, the *news*.

"How was your visit?" I managed, trying to keep this conversation on an expected track.

His gaze sobered, and he angled his head to the side, considering my question quietly for a few beats. "I'm really glad I went."

"Really?"

He nodded firmly. "I am. Obviously, I can't change the past, but..." He shrugged slightly. "My dad took responsibility for everything he could. Maybe it's because he's dying, but it still matters for me." Pain flared in his gaze briefly.

My hand, which was curled around his waist, clenched against him for a moment, as if I could absorb that pain for him. My heart gave an achy thump in my chest.

Kincaid took a slow breath. "If someone had asked me, what would your dad need to do or say for you to, I guess, accept his apology, I wouldn't have known how to answer. But he did what I needed."

"Wow," I said softly. "That's good."

One of his shoulders lifted slightly with another shrug. "It's bittersweet. I'm grateful, but... I can't undo what happened, and neither can he." He gave his head a little shake, and his attention refocused on me. "How was your weekend?"

I blinked up at him, feeling my lips curl into a smile because I was just so freaking happy he was home. "It was a weekend. I worked. Nothing amazing happened."

"How was work?" His lips teased at the corners, and my belly did a little shimmy.

"It was good." I chuckled softly, feeling unaccountably abashed—almost nervous—at just how happy I was that he was here with me.

Although the buzz of him being here felt so good, in a back corner of my thoughts was the reality that I had to tell him something big. Really big. I didn't know how he was going to feel about it. I still didn't know how *I* felt about it. I had gone from ninety-eight percent sure I wanted this baby to ninety-nine percent sure, and yet the clock was ticking. I had to tell Kincaid about the situation and soon.

My doubts were burgeoning because his presence made it all so very real. It was no longer just me counting on someone and learning to trust someone, but our hypothetical baby, an eventual child.

"I'm glad you're home," I said, my words feeling inadequate for the moment.

"I am, too," he murmured, his familiar voice, the low rumble of it, sliding over me like a soothing balm along my nerve endings.

He dropped his forehead to mine, his hand shifting from teasing through my hair lightly to sliding up to cup my nape. "Missed you, Tori," he murmured against my lips, each word shaping a promise.

Before I could take another breath, he was kissing me, and I was kissing him back with need spinning like liquid fire through my veins. We tumbled into the force of our desire, swept into a current.

The following morning, we showered together. My sated body, the one Kincaid had played like his own personal instrument the night before, sang for him yet again. I was starting to wonder if I could ever get enough of him.

After we got dressed, he came outside with me while I took Bella out. I still called it a walk with her, but these days it was more of a meander of slow, lazy loops around the yard. When we came back inside, after I made us coffee, we sat at the kitchen table.

His gaze sobered as he looked over at me. "I need to tell you something," he began.

My pulse immediately sped up, kicking along faster. My chest tightened, my heart feeling like it was trying to escape from the anxiety churning inside me. "Okay," I said carefully.

Kincaid took a quick gulp of his coffee, his eyes locking with mine. "I'm in love with you," he said.

Joy rose inside of me, as if bells ringing in unison, announcing to the world its presence and power.

"I love you," he repeated, his tone low and clear.

For this moment, I forgot all the reasons I was afraid. Tears splashed down my cheeks. "I love you, too," I whispered hoarsely.

He reached for my hands. "Are you okay?"

I nodded, though I couldn't quite speak for a few seconds. "Yeah, I just..." I cleared my throat, blinking the tears away. His touch grounded me and slowed the spinning sensation inside. "I just didn't expect any of this."

"I didn't either. Meeting my dad brought home how important it is to tell people what you're feeling. Especially when it matters."

"Was he in love with your mom?" I asked, the question slipping out before I could second-guess it.

He paused before he shook his head a little. "I think they liked each other a lot, but they were young. He talked about how, if he'd known she was pregnant before he was stationed somewhere else, he might have handled things differently. He understands now what's important and what it means to show up." He let out a breath and looked back at me. "I'm ballpark ten years older than he was when all of that happened. I like to think I'm older and wiser, maybe at least a little bit." He paused, as if gathering his thoughts. "I don't know what's going to happen with us. But I didn't want to let myself get in the way and let how important you are to me slide by just because I didn't expect it."

We stared at each other across the table. While my heart pounded along, his last sentence echoed in my mind. Because it wasn't just Kincaid I didn't expect.

# Chapter Thirty-One

# KINCAID

## A few days later

It had felt right to tell Tori how I felt, and yet, something between us felt off over the following days. I didn't know what it was. It wasn't as if she was treating me differently. It was more like a fragment of dust drifting through the air, or a smear on a window, just enough to mar the view when the light struck it just so. You wouldn't notice unless you tilted your head and looked from the right angle. Even if you could barely see it, it was there.

One morning, I stopped by Firehouse Café on my way into the station. Tish and Griffin were ahead of me in line. "Hey, hey," Griffin said when he saw me.

I hitched my brows up. "Hey, hey."

"Coffee and breakfast?" he asked.

"Of course. I'm getting donuts for the station."

"How many boxes, though?" Tish teased, one brow raised.

"Enough," I countered with a grin.

"How many is enough?" she pressed.

Griffin chuckled. "Two, maybe three, boxes."

"You better hope Luna has enough for you," she pointed out.

"I'm optimistic," I replied.

When Tish's gaze caught mine again, something flickered there. "How's Tori?" she asked.

"Good," I said. "Why do you ask?"

"She's my friend," Tish said simply, like that explained everything.

Maybe it did. This was a small town. People asked nosy questions. But there was something more behind her question. I could feel it.

Griffin looked between us. "You know how this goes."

"How what goes?"

"The curiosity of everyone in a small town," he said with a shrug.

Just then, the bell above the door jingled, and Beck, Graham, and Parker came walking in. "Hey there," Beck said, stepping in line behind us.

"You guys should get some donuts," I joked.

The conversation shifted to a teasing debate on who should pay for the donuts for the crews at the station. The debate carried all the way to the counter, where Luna appeared from the back with a stack of three donut boxes in her arms.

"I think Parker should get those," I offered helpfully.

Parker glanced among us, shaking his head. "Absolutely not." Luna's cheeks turned pink when he leaned across the counter and kissed her.

We ended up splitting the cost. After we had our coffees in hand, we headed off to the station. That afternoon, after work, I headed home. There was some construction on Main Street to repair a drainage ditch, and I had to detour through some side roads. That's when I passed the local medical office and saw Tori's car parked there.

Seeing her car there caught me off guard. We'd been spending almost every night together since I got back. I figured if she had a doctor's appointment, she might've mentioned it. A flicker of unease slid through me.

Later that evening, I pulled into her driveway. She was outside in the yard with Bella, and I got my usual greeting with Bella's trademark ecstatic tail wiggling and slow circles of joy. I crouched to pet her, stroking my palm down her back. When I straightened, I didn't mean to ask the question the way it came out. "What were you doing at the doctor's office today?"

Tori's eyes went wide. "Well," she finally said. "I could ask why you're asking."

I shrugged, holding my hands up. "It was the construction downtown. I had to drive around, and I saw your car in the parking lot. I wasn't stalking you, I swear."

She gave a little nod. "I didn't think you were."

"So, uh, is everything okay?" I asked, watching her carefully.

She blinked quickly, chewing the inside of one of her cheeks as she eyed me. "Um." Her voice wavered. "We need to talk."

"Okaaay," I said slowly. "About what?"

She hesitated, twisting her hands together. I waited, my jaw starting to tighten.

She straightened her shoulders and lifted her chin. "I'm pregnant."

# Chapter Thirty-Two

# TORI

*I'm pregnant.*

I could hear the echo of those two words ricocheting through my thoughts. Kincaid stared at me.

His eyes were wide, and his shoulders were stiff. The silence between us stretched so long I thought I might crack inside.

"What?" he finally said, his voice low and tense.

I swallowed, anxiety spinning like a storm in my chest. "I'm pregnant," I repeated. With my hands already twisted together, all I could do was tighten my grip, as if holding onto myself. "Um, and I'm telling you."

I watched as his shoulders rose with a slow, measured breath. He let it out all at once, running both hands through his hair before dropping them to his sides. "How long have you known?"

"What do you mean?" I hedged.

He pressed his tongue into his cheek and pinched the bridge of his nose. When his hand dropped, his gaze locked with mine again. "I don't know why, but something felt off between us. I've had this feeling for days. I was just wondering if this was what it was."

I nodded slowly, my anxiety clamoring even more loudly inside. "I didn't expect this," I blurted. "I didn't know what to do, and obviously..." My words trailed off as I paced a tight little circle before turning back to face him. "We used birth control," I added lamely.

"I know," he said. "It's not foolproof. Obviously."

His tone was sharper than I expected, sharp enough to feel as if it sliced the air between us.

"Kincaid, what the hell?" Anger flared in me now. "I just needed time to process. You've been gone."

"Is that when you found out?"

"Yeah." I exhaled shakily. "I wasn't sure what I wanted to do because, as we've established, this was unexpected."

"You could've talked to me," he said, his voice low but firm.

"I'm talking to you now!" I threw both hands in the air and let them fall again. I paced in another tight circle, as if the motion could burn through the panic inside me. "Look, this whole thing—not just being pregnant, but everything—has been a surprise for me. I never, ever, planned to be serious with anyone. I didn't expect to fall in love with you. I don't—" I stopped, swallowing through the tightness in my chest and throat. "I don't trust anyone."

"Anyone?" His voice lifted, sharp again.

I stopped pacing. "I trust my friends. I trust you, kind of. But when it comes to this? Commitment and all that? No. I don't trust in that. I hope you don't take that personally."

He clasped the back of his neck, his head bowing for a second. When he lifted his gaze to mine again, pain flickered in his eyes. "So there's no chance you're going to trust me?" He didn't sound angry anymore. He sounded hurt. "I'm just trying to clarify."

"I trusted my father," I whispered. "And, look what that got me." My voice cracked. "Ten years of lies. Most of my childhood, honestly. I found out when I was sixteen. The affair had been going on since I was six." My voice trembled, my hands shaking. "Shelly was like a second mom to me." My eyes stung with tears, and I swung my gaze away from his.

"Tori," he said softly. "I'm not your dad."

"I know, I just—"

"I would never do that to anyone. *Ever*."

"You don't know that—"

"I do." His voice was firm. "Maybe it's different for you, but I didn't have a father. Not really. And now I do—well, I guess I always did—but I didn't know him. If there's one thing I've learned due to not having my father around for most of my life, it's this: I would never build a life of lies like your father did. Maybe I can't promise you everything will be perfect, but I can promise I won't lie."

"Kincaid, I didn't mean to hurt you."

"I understand where you're coming from. But it would've been nice to know a little sooner that there's no chance you'd ever trust me." His voice frayed with the last two words. Without another, he turned and walked away.

———

I kept replaying the look in Kincaid's eyes. The pain contained there. Not anger. Not resentment. Just hurt. The way he looked at me before he walked away had cracked something inside me.

I'd been frozen in place, my feet stuck to the ground beneath them.

"Oh my God," I whispered into the silence.

Bella, who'd been sniffing along the edge of the yard, came to press her head against the side of my hip. Her little tail gave a slow wag. "I know, sweetie," I murmured, sweeping my palm over her back. "I screwed up."

She wiggled a little, her cloudy gaze peering up at me like she could see straight into my soul. I knew I had screwed up. And now, I had no idea what would happen next.

I didn't know how to square the fact that I didn't know how to trust anybody in a romantic relationship. The worst part was that I knew Kincaid wasn't like my dad. I knew he wouldn't do what my father did. But that didn't stop the confusion of my emotions from wrapping around me like fog. I couldn't see clearly.

I felt like I was the broken piece. If I'd been a different kind of daughter—maybe better, quieter, less complicated—then maybe my dad would've thought twice. Maybe he would've cared more about how much his actions and the eventual implosion of our family would hurt me and would carve a deep gash into my belief in others.

I didn't know what to do. "What do I do, Bella?" I whispered as I plunked down on the couch a little while later.

She gave another small tail wag, her presence always comforting and loyal.

I barely slept that night. I kept replaying the conversation with Kincaid, over and over. Every single time, it ended the exact same way, with him walking away and the pain in his gaze etched on my heart.

When the sun finally rose, I was too tired and restless to stay in bed. I got up, bundled myself into a sweatshirt, and loaded Bella into the passenger seat. We drove into town for coffee.

Casey and Luna were there. Firehouse Café was quiet and cozy. When I told them what happened, they both assured me they understood and it would be okay.

"I don't know what to do," I murmured, trying not to sigh again.

Casey handed my decaf coffee over the counter and waved off my attempt to pay. "We do consultations now. It's on the house."

I rolled my eyes. "No, really—" I tried to push the money across the counter, but Luna just nodded toward the tip jar. I stuffed the cash in there.

"You want a donut?" Luna asked.

"I can't even eat." I stared down at my decaf coffee. I'd gone with decaf ever since I'd found out I was pregnant.

"What do *you* want to do?" Casey asked gently.

"I want everything to be okay."

"Then, maybe," she said gently, "you should try talking to Kincaid again."

I hesitated. "I do trust him. I *think* I do. I feel terrible. He's really hurt, and I don't know how to fix that."

Luna raised an eyebrow, her smile kind as she studied me. "It kind of seems like you do know how. Life is messy, and it can be hard to trust, but there can also be people you do trust. Both things can exist at the same time."

I let out a gust of breath. "But how do I know it's going to be okay?"

"You don't," Casey said simply.

I blinked at her. "Well, that's not great."

She grinned a little. "No, but it's honest."

I took a sip of my completely unsatisfying decaf coffee.

"You know," Casey added, "Leo and I got together all because of a therapy appointment."

"I love that story. What does that have to do with this?" I asked.

"Well, Delaney—you know, our therapist—she told us something that stuck with me."

"Okay..."

"She said that in relationships, there are no guarantees. Ever. You don't know how it'll all go. So all you can do is learn to trust the big things. Like you love each other and you'll both keep trying to do your best, that kind of big thing."

I eyed her. "That's it?"

"She makes it sound smarter," Casey said with a shrug. "But yeah. Sometimes it helps just to have someone outside of your own head show you the way out of the weeds. If you overthink and want everything to always be okay, you're pretty much guaranteed to get tangled in the weeds."

"There is no guarantee," Luna chimed in. "You know that already. But not everyone's going to do what your dad did. Most people don't."

I closed my eyes for a second. "Fine, fine..." I took a breath when I looked at them again. "Kincaid's not even talking to me," I said quietly. "I sent him a text last night. He hasn't replied."

"I don't think that's about you not telling him right away," Luna said gently. "You needed time to figure it out, and he was out of town when you found out. That part makes sense."

"I think it's the trust part," Casey said, her voice clear. "You pretty much told him you couldn't trust him."

"I didn't say it like that—" I began before snapping my mouth shut.

"But it sounded like that," she said.

"It's just that I don't have faith in the universe. I don't have faith in life."

Casey nodded slowly. "I get that. But maybe this is your opportunity to give the universe a chance."

I snorted. "What does that mean?"

"This isn't therapy or logic or science. Just... a feeling. Like maybe you've already been given your one big hurt. You know? The one that breaks something deep."

I stared at her, feeling a stillness inside. "Go on..."

"Well, what your father did was rough. The betrayal to you and your mom, the devastation to your family. Kincaid isn't going to do that. Maybe this is your chance to believe in something and someone again."

Luna nodded along. "He already told you he loves you."

"And," Casey added, "he moved here because his mom wanted to come back to Alaska. He left behind his whole life to support her. You think *that* man's going to bail on you?"

I blinked hard, my throat tightening. I didn't know what I was going to do yet. But maybe I knew where to start.

"She wanted Kincaid to reconnect with where he was born. She loved it here. She wanted him to find his dad, and he did," Casey continued. "The man bought a house with a mother-in-law apartment solely so he could take care of his mom. There aren't a lot of people who would do that."

"I don't know if I would do that. It's a huge commitment," Luna said quietly.

Casey nodded. "Totally."

"I know he's a good man," I murmured.

"So, talk to Kincaid, talk this through. Give him a chance. Give the universe a chance," Luna said.

A few customers came in, and I slipped over to sit at an empty table. I was startled when I heard my name. I knew that voice. It was Shelly. I took a moment to gauge my body's reaction. That old, stinging anger wasn't even there anymore. I glanced over, offering a polite smile. "Hi, Shelly."

"Do you mind if I say something?" she asked.

"Go for it," I replied with a shrug.

"I couldn't help but overhear."

I glanced around the café. Other than the new customers who'd just walked in, it wasn't too crowded, so it was quiet enough to hear most of the conversation at the counter. "I didn't realize you were here."

"I figured," she said dryly. "Look, it's none of my business."

"Oh, it's definitely not," I countered.

"I know it's not," she continued. "But as someone who has completely screwed up with people who mattered to me a lot, I might have more experience in understanding your situation than most."

"I haven't done anything like what you did," I said slowly.

"Oh, no, no. That's not what I mean. I'm talking about living with regret." Her eyes were shining with tears. "I don't know the answer for you, and I don't really know Kincaid. He sounds like a nice man. What I do know is this: if I could go back and do it all over again and try to work through the things I was struggling with—my own marriage falling apart, honestly being envious of what your mom and dad had—I would've taken the time to find my way through it all. I totally understand why you don't trust people. Your father betrayed you, and I betrayed you, and we both betrayed your mother, and both of our families." Her voice caught. "I will live with that for the rest of my life, and I can't fix it. I can't change what I did. All I can do is own it and try to be accountable."

She paused, drawing a shaky breath. "In no way is your situation like that. But there is a kernel in common: not knowing what to do with those painful feelings, and not talking it through with the people you need to talk it through with, when you have the time to do it. So maybe do that. Especially if you plan to keep this baby."

I stared at her, the truth of what she was saying slamming into my heart. "Oh," I finally said.

For a minute, I was angry because she was right and I knew it. But she wasn't telling me anything that Casey and Luna hadn't just told me. She was just sharing it from the perspective of someone who had lost a lot and had to carry that regret. "Thank you," I finally said.

She let out a dry laugh. "You're welcome."

I started to turn and get up before I glanced back. "For what it's worth," I said, "I hope you're okay, and I hope you and Michelle find a way to get back to a better place."

"I do too." Her smile was sad and a little tight.

I stood from the table and slipped by her. Stepping outside, I pulled out my phone and texted Kincaid.

*I'm sorry. Unreservedly. I'm not sorry for waiting to tell you about being pregnant, because I needed time to process that, and you were out of town. But I am sorry for not being honest with you about how mixed up I am about trust. I do trust you. I do believe in you, and I do want a chance for us to make this work. Let me know when you're ready to talk. I love you.*

# Chapter Thirty-Three

# KINCAID

I reread Tori's text, and the last words blurred as I took them in.

I was standing in my mom's small kitchen, waiting for her. She had gone to her bedroom to get her purse, and I was so emotionally discombobulated I didn't even hear her come back in.

"Are you okay?" Her voice cut through my thoughts, and I spun around.

"Yeah."

She tipped her head slightly. "What is it?"

I took a steadying breath. "We have a doctor's appointment. Let's go."

My mother rolled her eyes but didn't say more. She followed me outside. Once she was situated in my truck, I summarized Tori's message. I'd already told her Tori was pregnant.

"Give her a chance," she said without hesitation. "I know you're hurt. But she's been through a lot."

"I know, but—"

"Kincaid." Her voice sharpened. "You were a stubborn boy. You always were, and now you are sometimes a stubborn man. She looked over at me, her gaze steady. "I was in her shoes once. I didn't expect to get pregnant. But I did." She paused for a moment, her tone softer when she spoke again.. "And, at that point, your father was already gone. It was before the era when cell phones were ubiquitous. I did try to find him, but it wasn't easy. Give Tori an opportunity to talk. I raised you. You're worth trusting. From what it sounds like, she knows that too. But given what you told me about what happened in her family, well..." She let out a breath. "That's a doozy. It's really hurtful. Two people who should have been some of the most trustworthy people in her life blew her world to smithereens."

I stared at the windshield, my jaw tight. "Okay," I said after a long silence. "I'll talk to her."

"I hope so. If she's planning on having this baby, you're going to have to figure this out."

The mere thought of that nearly sent me spinning into a panic. A baby. Ours. And yet, despite that flash of panic, I still felt, well, stubborn and not quite ready to talk to her.

I didn't know how to start. I was still so hurt at her instinctual lack of faith in me. It lingered under my skin like a bruise I couldn't stop pressing. I finally replied to her text.

*I just need a little more time.*

That was all I said, and I knew it wasn't enough.

# Chapter Thirty-Four

# TORI

Three entire freaking days passed, and I still hadn't heard more from Kincaid beyond his curt text.

"How long do you think I should keep waiting?" I asked.

Tish stared at me, a small wrinkle between her brows. "I don't know. Just give him a little more time."

Tish's suggestion boomeranged through my brain over the following days. Actually, three more days, which made it six days. Not that I was counting or anything. All the while, I was absolutely obsessing over how long was enough time.

That night—yes, the sixth night—Bella was breathing heavily after our walk. When we came back inside, she started pacing in rapid circles through the kitchen and living room. Worry spun wild inside of me. She was my best friend, the companion who was always there with unconditional love. I called the vet.

Since it was after business hours, I got an answering service. They assured me there was a vet on call and I'd hear back within fifteen minutes. "If you're that concerned," the woman on the phone said, "I'd recommend driving to the vet clinic. If they decide she needs to be seen, that's where they'll meet you."

"Okay, okay, okay," I repeated, trying not to panic.

Bella was still panting, her sides heaving like she couldn't get enough air. She looked like she might collapse right in front of me. While she kept on pacing, I threw on something that qualified as actual clothes, stuffed my feet into my tennis shoes, grabbed my purse, and raced outside to start my car. I planned to get the car ready and come back inside to get Bella.

"No, no, no," I muttered as the engine turned over and sputtered. I leaned my head back against the seat, closing my eyes and taking a slow breath.

I patted the dashboard gently, trying to be kind to my car. "You can start," I whispered.

The car did not, in fact, start. "Oh, no. No, no, no, no." I was on the verge of tears.

My phone vibrated in my pocket, and I fumbled to pull it out. "Hi!" I blurted the moment I saw the Willow Brook Veterinary Clinic flash across the screen. I'd been there enough with Bella that I kept it in my contacts.

"Hi, Tori," came Alice's calm voice. "I'm on call tonight."

"Oh, thank God. Bella's not breathing well. She's panting really hard. What should I do?"

"You should meet me at the clinic," Alice said without missing a beat. "We'll check on her and sort out what's going on."

"Okay. When should I meet you there?"

"I can make it in about twenty minutes. Does that work?"

"Yes. I'll be there." I hung up, heart pounding.

I tried one more time to start my car. "Maybe third time's the charm?"

No such luck. With my anxiety for Bella creating a cacophony in my thoughts, I wasn't thinking clearly when I called Kincaid. The phone rang and rang and rang before it went to voicemail.

My heart plunged into my stomach, but I marshaled enough composure to speak.

"Hey, um, I know maybe you don't want to talk to me now, or ever, but I'm in a bit of a bind. Maybe this isn't the right reason to call you, but you're the first person I thought to call. Bella's having trouble breathing, and I need to take her to the vet, and my car won't start, and I miss you..."

My voice cracked, and I had to blink through tears to see when I ended the call. I tried starting my car again. Still nothing. I scrambled out and ran back inside. Bella was in the kitchen now, not pacing, just standing there with her sides heaving.

"Oh, sweetie." I dropped to my knees beside her. "I'm going to get you there, one way or another."

I didn't want to waste time. The vet clinic was only about ten minutes away. I glanced at my watch and called my mom.

"Hey, honey," she answered.

"Hey. Sorry to bother you, but Bella's having trouble breathing and I need to take her to the vet. My car won't start. It's probably my battery or something."

"Okay, I can—"

My phone buzzed in my hand again. "Hang on, Mom. I'll call you right back. Kincaid's on the other line."

"You got it."

I switched over to the other call. "Hey."

"I can give you a ride," Kincaid said. His voice was careful, but clear.

"Are you sure?"

"Positive. I'm already on my way over."

"Oh, thank God. Really?"

"Of course, really. Also, you can just thank me and not God," he teased lightly.

A watery laugh bubbled up in my throat. "Okay. I'll see you in a few minutes. Thank you so much."

As soon as he hung up, I burst into tears. The emotions felt like a tidal wave inside. There was Bella and Kincaid, and this whole mess I had made.

I took a shaky breath. "Okay, girl, are you ready?" I looked down at my dog.

Her breath was still heaving, but she met my eyes, and my

heart ached. I would do anything for this sweet girl. She was my best friend. She'd been with me through so much.

Just a matter of minutes later, I'd updated my mom that I didn't need a ride when I heard the sound of tires crunching over gravel, and I headed outside. Bella seemed more uncomfortable when I tried to carry her, so I let her walk slowly at my side.

Kincaid was out of his truck in a flash. "Hey, sweet girl," he murmured as he knelt in front of her. "We got you. Should I pick her up?" he asked, glancing at me.

"I don't know. She seemed more comfortable when I let her walk, but obviously, we have to pick her up to get her in your truck."

"I'll be careful."

We watched her make her way carefully over to his truck before he gently lifted her into the small cab behind the front seats. A few moments later, we were on the road. It was late enough that the sky had dimmed to twilight. A crescent moon was rising above the mountains, casting a soft glow over the last of the lingering snow.

"Thank you," I said into the quiet.

"Of course." He hesitated before adding, "I've been meaning to call you anyway."

"You have?" My eyes jerked toward his profile.

"I have," he said simply. "Let's talk later, though."

I reflexively glanced toward Bella in the back seat. She was sitting up, alert and watching out the window. Her breathing still sounded labored.

"I don't know what's wrong with her."

"I'm sure it'll be fine."

"She's not young," I replied, anxiety for her twisting my heart sharply.

"No, but she's still eating and drinking okay, right?" he asked. The worry in his voice helped me not feel so alone in mine.

"Yeah. She is."

The rest of the short drive passed in silence. We pulled into the gravel lot behind the veterinary clinic. The building was mostly dark, and I started to fret. Before I could spiral too far, headlights swung into the lot, and Alice waved as she hopped out of her car.

Kincaid and I got out as she called, "Just come in the back with me."

She hustled ahead, flipping on lights as she went. By the time we caught up in the hallway with Bella, Alice immediately crouched down at her side.

"Is it getting any better?" she asked. I'd grown up with Alice in Willow Brook, although she'd been a few years ahead of me in school. I was grateful she'd taken over the vet clinic here when she moved back to town.

I pulled out my phone. "I took a video at home. Here—watch."

Alice studied it quickly and nodded. "Okay, yeah. She already sounds better, and I know what's going on."

"You do?"

Bella had stopped pacing. Her breathing was still labored, but it had eased a little.

"It's tracheal collapse."

"What does that mean? Is she going to die?" I pressed.

"She's not going to die, not at this moment," Alice said calmly. "But it's uncomfortable. Usually, they just need a little time to recover. If it doesn't ease up, there are things we can do."

"I'm going to give her some medicine. It'll relax her a little. The muscles supporting the trachea weaken with age, and some-times it collapses like this. They can't get enough air, so they try harder, but they don't have the muscular strength to make it work. So it just gets worse. Until they can get out of the cycle of breathing like that."

"Oh, my God..." I sagged against the wall, swiping at the tears tracking down my face.

Alice's lips curled into a soft smile. "We can get Bella through this."

"Did I just waste your time? I made you come all the way in."

"Absolutely not. Even if you'd texted me that video, I would have wanted to see her. She's not young, but she's doing pretty well for her age."

"Is she really?" I asked quietly.

Alice looked from Bella to me to Kincaid, then nodded. "She is. I don't think we're losing her yet. She might be mostly blind and deaf, but her heart's still pretty strong. Sometimes things like this happen just because she's old. That's it."

"I just want her to be comfortable."

"That's what we're going to do." She stood, glancing toward the exam rooms. "Let me do an exam to cover all the bases. Just a quick check, but first I'm going to get those meds."

We walked through the open doorway Alice pointed to, and I knelt down beside Bella. I stroked the soft fur just over her forehead. She tipped her head up and closed her eyes. She loved any and all affection. "That's my sweet girl," I whispered. Her tail gave a little wag.

"She's going to be okay," Kincaid said softly.

I smiled up at him. "I know. She's just old, and trust me, she already sounds much better."

"Oh, I heard the video. She didn't sound good at all."

Alice reappeared a moment later, holding out a small bottle. "This is just going to chill her out a little bit, okay? It's an anxiety medication. Just enough to take the edge off so she can relax if she gets stressed. Because not being able to breathe is stressful."

"For all of us," I murmured.

Alice chuckled softly. I moved to lift Bella onto the exam table, but Alice shook her head and dropped to the floor beside her. "No need."

She listened to Bella's heart and lungs, carefully checked her body, and gave her several treats. Bella licked her hand like the good girl she was. "Even since you've been here, she's improved," Alice said.

"How long does it normally last if it happens again?" I asked.

"Sometimes just a few minutes. Sometimes longer. But now you know what's happening. You can always call us, or just hop in the car and start driving. Whoever's on call will meet you here. We love this girl," she added.

"We do," Kincaid agreed.

Alice's eyes caught his, her smile softening. "Bella's a very good girl."

"The best," I said stoutly, because she absolutely was.

After that, Alice walked us out to the parking lot. When I apologized again for dragging her here, she shook her head. "All right. Stop apologizing. We have on-call services for exactly these reasons. It's much easier for us to make a clear diagnosis if we see a pet when something's happening."

A few minutes later, we were on the road again, headed back to my place. I glanced over my shoulder and felt a rush of relief as I saw Bella settle in and actually lie down. I let out a heavy breath. "Oh, wow. I think she's going to be okay."

Kincaid reached across the console and laced his fingers through mine. "Alice said she was. So she is."

I squeezed his hand. My stomach was still full of nervous energy, and now that the mini-crisis was over, all my other doubts came roaring back. "I'm sorry," I blurted out without any lead-in.

"You don't need to apologize. I needed a little time to think things over, and maybe I took too long. My mom gave me a lecture."

A startled laugh slipped out of me. "Your mom gave you a lecture?"

"Yeah. She said she'd been where you were—unplanned pregnancy and all—and it wasn't fair for me to expect you to tell me right away."

"I know, but I should've been more honest about how much I struggle with trust."

"It's not that I don't understand, Tori. I guess I let my pride get in the way. I took it really personally."

My laugh was a little bitter. "Well, I mean, it *is* personal. We've been together, and I love you, and I never bothered to mention that I wasn't so sure I knew how to do this trust thing. Which is kind of important for a relationship."

"I hope you can give me a chance to earn your trust." His tone was low and solemn, and my heart felt cracked.

"It's not you," I said quietly. "You have earned my trust. You know who helped me figure that out?"

"Uh, no..." he said slowly.

"Shelly."

"Shelly?" His gaze briefly flicked toward me, his eyes wide and startled, before shifting back to the road.

"Yeah, go figure. She overheard me talking to Luna and Casey at the café. She told me she knew a thing or two about regret and not saying what needed to be said. I talked to my mom, and she pointed out that either I go through life assuming it's always going to blow up, or I give people a chance, knowing there are no guarantees. I freaking hate that, by the way. I'd like a guarantee or two in life."

The soft laugh that rumbled in his chest eased the tension in my own. His thumb brushed slowly along the inside of my wrist in a soothing pass. "Right? That does suck. I'm on board with that. We need guarantees."

"There are no more guarantees," I said. "Companies don't even guarantee their products anymore."

His shoulders shook with another laugh. "No, they don't."

"So, I know you can't promise me anything."

"Actually," he said. "I can."

"What do you mean? We just agreed there are no guarantees."

"I know," Kincaid began, "but I can promise you that I'm not going to do something like your dad did. I don't know your dad, and I don't know what was going on with him and your mom, but that's not something I would ever let happen."

As he rolled to a stop in front of my house, I turned to face

Kincaid. His eyes met mine, steady and clear. My heart thumped along, the beat steady and true. Because while I knew life didn't offer guarantees, I also knew this to be true: Kincaid was a good man.

I didn't know what I'd missed about my dad. My mom might never know either. But whatever it was, it had to do with a lack of commitment and a lack of honesty when things were challenging.

I knew beyond all doubts—and I had those in surplus—that Kincaid knew how to uphold a commitment and to be honest even when it wasn't easy. "I know," I whispered.

"Now," he said, "let's get Bella inside. Should I carry her?"

We both glanced to the back seat. Bella was sound asleep, her head on her paws, her breathing soft and even. "Let's see if she needs a bathroom break."

After Bella took care of business, we got her settled inside, and she curled up in her bed with a contented sigh.

Kincaid's eyes found mine, and he reached for my hand. "I missed you."

When he pulled me into his arms, I felt like I was coming home. This connection between us, it was just for us. It felt real and true. No matter what, I knew this feeling would buoy me through the hard days when they came, just as I hoped it would for him.

"I don't mean for this to be all about sex," he murmured, his breath warm against my ear before we leaned back to look at each other.

A giggle slipped out. "I don't mean for it to be either, but I missed you. A lot."

His chuckle rumbled through me, the sound low and delicious. I reached for his hand again, leading him upstairs. A little while later, when I sank down over him, sheathing him inside my channel and locked in the heat of his dark gaze, everything felt just right.

Chapter Thirty-Five

# KINCAID

My awareness filtered in slowly. It was hazy at first as I cataloged the sensations around me. The feel of Tori, warm and soft, curled against me. The sound of her steady breathing. And, of course, Bella's familiar snoring from the floor nearby.

My lips curled into a smile as I slowly opened my eyes. All was well, and all felt right with the world. I took a quiet, deep breath, not wanting to wake Tori. My fingers sifted through her hair. My thoughts drifted lazily to the evening before.

I felt it when she stirred awake—a soft hum of awareness buzzing between us. Her lips moved against the curve of my shoulder, where her head was tucked. "Good morning," she said.

I chuckled. "Good morning."

Before we could say another word, the sound of Bella's paws clicking on the hardwood floor reached us. Tori giggled. "Bella's awake. No talking allowed if you don't want her to know we're up."

"Hey, you're the one who talked first," I teased.

She lifted her head and smiled at me. Just like that, my heart flipped in my chest. The poignancy of the moment hit me hard —how simple it was, how good it felt waking up beside Tori.

Knowing we'd take Bella out together. Realizing we had this ordinary, beautiful life starting to take shape between us.

I leaned close and kissed her, slow and fierce. "Let's take Bella out."

A few minutes later, we walked out into the cool morning. The air was damp and earthy, the breeze soft and quiet. A nearby owl called out from the trees, early or late to the owl, depending on how you looked at it. Bella happily did her business before trotting back to us, her tail wagging as she circled around our legs.

Tori's gaze shifted toward her car. "When should we jump-start my car?"

I shrugged. "Whenever you want."

"Now works," she said quickly. "You don't mind?" she added, her brows arching up as she looked up at me.

"Of course not."

Moments later, I'd pulled my truck up close to her little hatchback. We hooked up the cables and got her battery started. She bounced on her toes and kissed me on the cheek.

"That's all I get for jumpstarting your car?" I teased.

She shrugged, grinning. "I'm just grateful. Also, thank you again for the ride to the vet clinic last night."

"No need to thank me. You probably need a new battery," I pointed out.

"Yeah. I probably do. But that's a problem for another day."

"We can take care of it today. Either way, you should do a little drive today to give your battery some run time."

"I should?"

"Yeah."

"All right," Tori said with a shrug. "Should I take it for a little drive now?" She looked down at her tennis shoes. She was still wearing my T-shirt over her sweatpants—easily the best outfit I'd ever seen on her.

"Whenever you want."

"Let's go together."

We got Bella settled in the backseat and went for a little drive through the misty morning.

"Let's go to my favorite viewing spot," Tori said.

"You have a favorite viewing spot?"

She nodded, her lips curling in a slow smile when she glanced over. A few minutes later, she turned down a side road that led us up to a small parking area at the top of a rise. The overlook offered a sweeping view across the valley below—tall grasses with a stream winding through and the ocean visible in the distance. The grasses waved in the breeze as the sky turned shades of tangerine, gold, and soft pink.

We watched quietly while Bella sniffed every inch of the wooden railing at the edge of the overlook. I stole a quick glance at Tori. Her hair was still tousled, and her cheeks a little pink from the cool air. This wasn't just a beautiful morning. It was the beginning of more for us.

As the sun rose, its rays broke through the clouds and glinted on the stream below. We made our way back to her house, showered, and headed into town. Tori wanted coffee. We'd switched over to my truck, since the plan was to pick up a new battery for hers.

I felt her gaze on me before I flicked a glance toward her. "What is it?" I asked.

She took a quick breath. "When do we tell people about the baby?"

"Ohhh," I said slowly. "I figured I'd leave that up to you."

"It's not up to just me. It's your baby too," she pointed out.

"I know. But it just seems like, in this, I should defer to you. You're the one who's going to be, well, quite literally growing the baby."

She let out a quick breath. "I know. I don't know. Some people already know."

She had told me last night that she'd talked with Tish, Casey, and Luna. "Okay. So maybe we don't wait. If you're ready, I'm ready." When I pulled into the parking lot at Firehouse Café, I turned off the engine and looked over at her. "I just want to make sure this is what you want."

"What do you mean?" she asked, her brow furrowing.

"Having a baby. You can still change your mind."

She held my gaze for several long beats before she finally nodded. "I know, and I appreciate you saying that. But I'm ready. It feels right, and it feels right with you."

My heart gave a resounding kick against my ribs, as if in agreement with her—which was maybe odd, but that's exactly how it felt. I meant what I'd said: if Tori wasn't ready, I would've supported her, no matter what.

But the idea of having a family with Tori—who I loved— meant everything to me.

"I'm going to follow your lead," I told her.

She eyed me. "What do you mean?"

"Just that."

When I opened the café door and held it for her, motion caught my eye. I glanced over to see Griffin and Tish pulling in. Moments later, we were inside, standing in line. Janet happened to be at the counter. She was often there, but not always.

"What are you doing here so early?" I teased.

Janet flashed a grin. "I still like to come in early sometimes. Remind myself that getting up to be here by five-thirty has been a part of my life for—" She paused and let out a wondering laugh. "Oh, my gosh. Almost forty years."

"Is this the first time you've counted?" Tori asked.

Janet shrugged. "Oh, I think about it. It's just that saying it out loud makes me feel old."

"You're not old," Tori said stoutly, just as Luna walked out from the back.

"Janet is definitely not old," Luna announced.

Janet rolled her eyes. "I'm not young, but it's okay. I appreciate every year of my life. I've earned each one."

Griffin was already haggling with Luna over donuts. She put a hand on her hip and narrowed her eyes. "It's early. I need time to make more. You can only have one dozen. It's just me. I'm the only one here making them," she added pointedly.

Griffin chuckled. "Fine. I'll come back later."

Tori and Tish were talking quietly nearby, and Janet's gaze bounced toward them as she slid coffees across the counter. "Okay, what is it, ladies?" she asked, eyes narrowing in playful suspicion.

Tori looked nervous. Her eyes darted to me for a beat before she blurted out, "I'm pregnant."

Janet's brows hitched high before a wide smile cracked across her face. Within seconds, she was bustling around the counter, arms open for a hug. Tori laughed as Janet pulled her in and gave her a squeeze. When she stepped back, Janet's gaze arced to me. "I assume Kincaid is the father?"

"Yes," Tori said quickly. "Absolutely. We weren't planning it," she added, her voice even but a little breathy. "And, well, it's happening." She glanced around at the small group gathered near the counter. "We were obsessing over—or rather, I was obsessing over—when we should tell people. But I decided there was no sense in keeping it a secret."

"How far along are you?" Luna asked.

Tori paused. "I think... about twelve weeks now."

"Wow, congratulations," Griffin said.

"Maybe we weren't planning it," Tori added with a smile, "but we're rolling with it, and we feel good about it."

My lips tugged into a smile, my heart feeling cleaved open. Maybe I hadn't expected any of this, but it felt like a slice of joy. We would have to roll with it because I had no idea how to be a father, but I was ready to face it. With Tori.

Tori and Tish continued talking by the display case. Meanwhile, Griffin caught my gaze. His brows hitched up ever so slightly, the silent question clear in his eyes.

"I feel good about it," I said quietly, answering him.

He nodded. "Good. Sometimes curve balls are the best ones to catch."

I chuckled. "That's one way to put it."

I let my gaze slide over to Tori, who was now laughing at something Tish had said.

Bringing my focus back to Griffin, I added, "It just feels..." I paused, searching for the words. "I don't know, I guess, ready. I have no illusions. I know it won't be easy."

"But you love her," Griffin said, his voice low.

"I do," I said simply. "I really do."

*Chapter Thirty-Six*

# TORI

Kincaid and I were chatting at the counter when I heard his name. He glanced over his shoulder. "Oh, Mom, good to see you." He gestured to me. "You can meet Tori."

*Oh, my God.* This was fine, totally fine. I could meet his mom. I kind of needed to get this over with, but anxiety kicked up like an unexpected gust of wind swirling in my chest.

Kincaid's mom—his mom!—stopped beside him. Her eyes were kind, and I did my best to ignore my anxiety.

"I'm Tori." My voice came out like a croak. I cleared my throat. "It's so nice to meet you," I added as I extended my hand.

Claudia smiled warmly. "You as well."

Her eyes twinkled, and I had no idea what Kincaid might have already said about me. Before I knew it, he had somehow herded us over to a table.

"Are you glad to be back in Alaska?" I asked politely.

"I am," she replied. "Back when I was stationed in Anchorage with the Air Force, I came to visit Willow Brook a couple of times and absolutely loved it. I'm not really a city girl," she added. "And Anchorage is..."

"Definitely a city," I finished with a smile.

"Exactly! Most people don't realize how big it is, especially those who live out of state."

"I know," I said. "It's even bigger now."

She laughed softly. "That it is. Kincaid tells me you work at Fireweed Winery?"

Considering I was pregnant, and I knew she knew, it was kind of funny to tiptoe around that, but sometimes chatting about the mundane smoothed the way. "I do. I actually love it. I know waiting tables isn't anything spectacular, but I enjoy it." I rolled my eyes. "I went to college and got a degree in communication studies. Not exactly sure what I'm doing with it."

She shrugged. "You'll figure it out. A college degree isn't the end-all be-all."

"True," I said. "A friend who works with Fireweed Industries since they own the winery, and she mentioned there are opportunities for advancement. The guy who manages our location used to run the flagship restaurant in Fireweed Harbor. I might be able to take over his position when he transitions out."

"Sounds like you're building something," she said with a nod. "I'm all about doing what you enjoy."

Kincaid stepped away to use the restroom, so it was just the two of us for a moment. Janet came by our table and smiled between us. "How are you ladies doing?" she asked brightly.

Kincaid's mom beamed up at her. "We're good. Very good."

When Janet moved along, Claudia studied me for a beat before saying, "I'm thrilled for you and Kincaid."

Her words were soft, but clear, and I blinked away the tears that rose with the rush of emotion inside. "Thank you. It's unexpected, but we're excited."

A few minutes later, my mom came walking in, and we pulled over another chair so she could join us. I wasn't entirely sure how I felt about them meeting. It wasn't that I didn't want them to—it just made things feel *real* with Kincaid. Ever since I'd stumbled through telling him about being pregnant, I felt as if I was trying surf through wave after wave of uncertainty, which made me even more unsure of myself.

Later that afternoon, my mom called me about some mail she'd picked up in our shared post office box. "So, you met Kincaid's mother," she said casually.

"Yeah. You were there, Mom," I replied dryly.

"I know," she replied, and I could hear the grin in her voice. "But what does it mean about you and him?"

"Mom!" I sputtered. "We're having a baby!"

Her laugh came through the line like a breeze. "I know, I know. Just putting it out there that you could admit you love him out loud."

"I appreciate your feedback. I'll be by to pick up the mail later," I murmured before I ended the call to the sound of her laughter.

# EPILOGUE

## Tori

*Over a month later*

My foot bounced where my legs were crossed, tapping out an uneven rhythm that betrayed just how nervous I felt. Kincaid's hand slid over my thigh just before he caught mine, giving it a reassuring squeeze.

"Are you nervous?" he asked softly.

I slid my gaze to his, offering a sheepish smile as I lifted my other hand and held my thumb and forefinger apart with a tiny gap. "A little."

Just then, there was a light knock on the office door where we were waiting for the doctor. A familiar voice called, "Come in."

A moment later, the doctor stepped inside. "How are we doing? Feeling okay?" she asked, wheeling her stool over to sit across from us.

"I'm nervous," I blurted out before I could stop myself.

She offered a warm smile. "Of course. That's understandable. Pregnancy is such a common event that it's easy to make light of it, but growing an entire human in your body is kind of a big deal."

I nodded, trying to take a slow breath. My heart felt like it was thudding in my throat.

"Everything looks great," she continued. "Last time, you said you wanted to think on it..."

"We want to know," I cut in quickly.

She sputtered a soft laugh. "Okay then. It's a boy."

I pressed a hand to my chest as a rush of emotion slammed into me. Kincaid squeezed my hand tightly, and I could barely form words. "Wow," I finally managed.

"Wow," Kincaid echoed, sounding stunned.

She looked between the two of us. "Are we happy with that news?"

"Oh, we'd have been happy either way," I said quickly. "Which is why we wanted to know. This way we can plan."

"Now you can obsess over names," she teased. "I should add, everything else looks good."

"So everything is okay?" Kincaid pressed.

"Exactly. Your little boy is developing right on schedule, and he looks like he's going to be big. There's a range, and he's on the upper end of it."

Kincaid nodded along calmly, while I couldn't speak for a moment. My chest was tight, my throat knotted with emotion. Tears were stinging the corners of my eyes.

"Is there anything else we need to do today?" I finally asked, my voice a little hoarse.

"Not a thing," she said with a smile. "You've got all your appointments lined up and you can just call the office to schedule if anything unexpected comes up. But I don't anticipate that. You're healthy, and your baby is healthy." She looked between us again. "Any more questions for me?"

I glanced over at Kincaid. He raised his brows in question, and I gave my head a slight shake. "No, I don't think so."

"All right," she said, standing. "I'll see you at your next appointment."

Later that night, we were back at Kincaid's house. I was still working on calling it mine. I had officially moved in a few weeks ago. It made sense. He owned the house, and there was more space. His mom still lived in the in-law suite beside the main house, and Bella loved the fenced yard. He'd put a fence up just for her. Not that she ever wandered far, but she definitely enjoyed meandering on her own terms and sprawling out in the sunshine.

At the moment, she was napping beside the table on the back deck, the breeze rustling in the trees.

"What do you think?" Kincaid asked, lifting his glass of water and tipping it toward me. We had just finished dinner—grilled salmon with asparagus and sweet potatoes. I had quickly discovered that Kincaid was not only a solid cook but also pretty talented with the grill. His mom liked to tease that it was his "manly cooking."

I took a sip of my water and tilted my head. "I don't know. We could name him after your dad?"

"Seriously?" His brows hitched high. "What about your dad?"

The idea had been bouncing in my brain ever since we found out we were having a boy, and I knew that my dad would have been thrilled. But naming our son after him felt too emotionally complicated for me.

I shook my head decisively. "Too messy for me. I don't think I can do that."

"Whatever you think?" His tone lilted in question.

"We could name our baby after you," I replied.

He looked honestly shocked, his eyes going wide and brows slamming up to his hairline.

"People name their own kids after themselves all the time," I pointed out.

"True," he said, "but I feel weird about us having the same name. Then we have to do nicknames, and it just feels messy."

"Okay, okay," I said with a laugh.

I grinned. "Should we ask your mom and my mom? Wait," I

said suddenly, an idea clicking into place. "I know what we can do."

"What?"

"Let's name him after my granddad. First name, and then his middle name can be your name."

"What's your granddad's name?"

I hesitated, feeling my lips tug into a grin. "What if you just say yes, even if I don't tell you first?"

"Is it an awful name?"

I giggled. "No! I promise it's not. His name was Colson."

He studied me for a moment, a small smile playing on his lips. "I actually like that name," he said. "That works for me."

I beamed, reaching over to grab his hands and squeeze them tightly. "Good."

Bella seemed to sense the shift in the air. She stirred, stretching slowly from her napping spot on the deck and lifting her head.

"What do you think, girl?" I asked softly.

She wandered over, bumping her nose gently against my belly. She'd started doing that recently, and I was convinced she knew I was pregnant.

"Bella approves," Kincaid said with a teasing grin.

"I hope she makes it until the baby is born," I whispered.

"She will," he said, his voice quiet but certain.

I wanted to believe that, so much. Bella had been with me through so many events. She was my first girl. The idea of her not being around for every milestone of our lives elicited a echoing sense of loneliness.

"I love how much faith you have," I murmured.

He reached for my free hand, linking his fingers through mine. His touch was strong and sure. It steadied me.

"I kind of can't believe it," he said.

"Believe what?"

He met my eyes, his expression warm and serious all at once. "That I found you, and I fell in love with you. I sure as hell didn't expect that. And, now we're having a baby. I'm a little nervous, but I'm not freaked out. I think being nervous is normal."

I smiled. "I can't imagine not being nervous about a baby." My heart clenched. "I can't believe all of it either."

He smiled as Bella rested her chin on my knee. I reached down and stroked behind her ears, my heart full to bursting.

"I feel like we have a mini family," I said, savoring the feel of the breeze.

"We do." Kincaid nodded, his gaze landing on Bella snoozing at my feet. "We're three now, and we'll be four soon."

My shoulders rose as I took a slow breath. My hand swept in an arc across the yard, from Bella to him, and around the little world we were building.

"All of this," I murmured. "Just for us. It feels right. I didn't expect any of it either, but I'm so grateful."

# KINCAID

The following morning, I woke up before Tori and took Bella outside. Even though we'd only been here all together for a little while, Bella had adjusted beautifully. She'd even started coming to me in the mornings instead of waiting for Tori—almost as if she understood her person needed the extra rest. The vet said she was doing remarkably well for her age, and honestly, I hoped she'd stick around for a few more years.

After she did her business and we strolled back inside, Tori was standing in the kitchen, eyeing the coffee pot wistfully. "You're allowed one cup a day," I reminded her as I approached, looping my arms around her waist and pressing a kiss to her forehead.

She smiled up at me. "I know, but I've gotten used to not having it," she said with a little shrug.

We both looked down at her belly between us. "Are you ready for the baby shower?" I asked.

She looked up, shrugging slightly as a wondering laugh

slipped out. "I guess? It sounds elaborate, and I don't even know what to think."

"It'll be fun."

Her eyes twinkled as she arched a brow. "By the way, I love you."

I leaned in and gave her a lingering kiss, holding her close.

Thank you for reading Kincaid & Tori's story! Want a glimpse of the future for them? Join my newsletter to receive an exclusive scene.

Sign up here: https://BookHip.com/LVPHCGK

p.s. If you are already subscribed, you'll still be able to access the scene.

Up next is in the Wild Fire Series is Make It Last.

**Tanner rescued me from a glacier. I tried not to fall for him.**

After my divorce blows up in spectacular and humiliating fashion, a girls' trip to Alaska sounds like a solid escape. Until I break my ankle on a glacier and get rescued by a ridiculously hot firefighter.

I'm sooooo done with men. He's determined to change my mind.

Falling for him so fast my head is spinning is definitely not part of the plan.

One-click: Make It Last - due out late summer 2026!

For more swoon & sass...

This Crazy Love kicks off the Swoon Series - small town southern romance with enough heat to melt you! Jackson & Shay's story is epic - swoon-worthy & intensely emotional. Jackson just happens to be Shay's brother's best friend. He's also *seriously* easy on the eyes. Shay has a past, the kind of past she would most definitely like to forget. Past or not, Jackson is about to rock her world. Don't miss their story!

Burn For Me is a second chance romance for the ages. Sexy firefighters? Check. Rugged men? Check. Wrapped up together? Check. Brave the fire in this hot, small-town romance. Amelia & Cade were high school sweethearts & then it all fell apart. When they cross paths again, it's epic - don't miss Cade's story!

For more small town romance, take a visit to Last Frontier Lodge in Diamond Creek. A sexy, alpha SEAL meets his match with a brainy heroine in Take Me Home. Marley is all brains & Gage is all brawn. Sparks fly when their worlds collide. Don't miss Gage & Marley's story!

If sports romance lights your spark, check out The Play. Liam is a British footballer who falls for Olivia, his doctor. A twist of forbidden heats up this swoon-worthy & laugh-out-loud romance. Don't miss Liam & Olivia's story.

Be sure to sign up for my newsletter for the latest news, teasers & more! Click here to sign up: http://jhcroixauthor.com/subscribe/

When We Dare
Fake It True
Only Ever You
Just For Us
Make It Last - coming late summer 2026
**Heartfire Falls Series**
What We Keep
Mine To Hold
Be With Me - coming summer 2026!
**Fireweed Harbor Series**
Make You Mine
Dare To Fall
Be The One
One More Time
Wait For You
Ever After All
**Light My Fire Series**
Wild With You
Hold Me Now
Only Ever Us
Fall For Me
Keep Me Close
With Every Breath
All It Takes
Take Me Now
Meant To Be
**Dare With Me Series**
Crash Into You
Evers & Afters
Come To Me
Back To Us
Take Me There
After We Fall
**Swoon Series**
This Crazy Love

Wait For Me
Break My Fall
Truly Madly Mine
Still Go Crazy
If We Dare
Steal My Heart

**Into The Fire Series**

Burn For Me
Slow Burn
Burn So Bad
Hot Mess
Burn So Good
Sweet Fire
Play With Fire
Melt With You
Burn For You
Crash & Burn
That Snowy Night

**Haven's Bay Holiday Series**

All I Want
All I Need
All We Have
All We Are

**Brit Boys Sports Romance**

The Play
Big Win
Out Of Bounds
Play Me
Naughty Wish

**Diamond Creek Alaska Novels**

When Love Comes
Follow Love
Love Unbroken
Love Untamed
Tumble Into Love

<u>Christmas Nights</u>
**Lodge Series**
<u>Take Me Home</u>
<u>Love at Last</u>
<u>Just This Once</u>
<u>Falling Fast</u>
<u>Stay With Me</u>
<u>When We Fall</u>
<u>Hold Me Close</u>
<u>Crazy For You</u>
<u>Just Us</u>

# ACKNOWLEDGMENTS

To all of my readers, whether you've been reading my books for years or just found me with this story - thank you, thank you, thank you. It bears repeating when I contemplate how much gratitude I have for every reader who has taken a chance on my stories.

Gracious thanks to my editor for guiding me to make Kincaid and Tori's story better with each page, to Terri D. for patiently scouring for those pesky details. My early readers also send friendly notes about lingering errors, and I'm so grateful.

Najla Qamber continues to make magic with these covers. So much gratitude to my assistant, Erin, for helping me navigate the choppy waters of this author thing.

Much love to my family, my dogs, and my friends.

xoxo

J.H. Croix

# ABOUT THE AUTHOR

USA Today bestselling author J. H. Croix writes emotionally charged, small town Alaska romance with heat and heart featuring protective firefighter and first responder heroes and smart, strong heroines. Best known for her interconnected series set in Willow Brook, Alaska, Croix creates immersive fictional communities where the town itself becomes a character and found family is at the heart of every love story.

Having lived for over a decade in a tiny coastal Alaska town, Croix brings an authentic sense of place to her rugged mountain settings—where wildfire crews, stubborn alpha men, fiercely independent women, and tight-knit communities collide. Her interconnected series span multiple generations and friend groups, rewarding readers who love returning characters and layered small town worlds.

She lives in a small town with her husband and two spoiled dogs. When she's not writing swoony Alaska romance, she's cooking, counting birds in her backyard, or plotting her next romance while running with her dogs.

*Places you can find me:*
jhcroixauthor.com

facebook.com/jhcroix

instagram.com/jhcroix

bookbub.com/authors/j-h-croix

www.ingramcontent.com/pod-product-compliance
Lightning Source LLC
Chambersburg PA
CBHW032233050726
47591CB00001B/382